the UNFINISHED portrait

some stories are painted in love, loss, and memories

ABHISHEK BHATT

BlueRoseONE.com
Stories Matter
NewDelhi • London

BLUEROSE PUBLISHERS
India | U.K.

For permissions requests or inquiries regarding this publication, please contact:

BLUEROSE PUBLISHERS
www.BlueRoseONE.com
info@bluerosepublishers.com
+91 8882 898 898
+4407342408967

ISBN: 978-93-6783-826-6

Cover design: Abhishek Bhatt
Typesetting: Namrata Saini

First Edition: January 2025

Gratitude

As I often say, every person carries within them countless stories—some bitter, some sweet. Through this book, I want to express my heartfelt gratitude to Lord Shiva for blessing me with beautiful memories and the gift of transforming my thoughts into stories that I can share with all of you.

Kedarnath Dham holds a deeply significant place in my life, and its divine essence has inspired this tale. Through these pages, I've tried to weave its charm into a story that's close to my heart—a sweet and simple love story that I hope you will cherish as much as I enjoyed creating it.

To Lord Shiva, my eternal guide and inspiration, I bow in gratitude.

Acknowledgement

To all the souls I've crossed paths with, each of you a thread woven into the intricate fabric of my life. Every fleeting interaction, whether sweet or bitter, carries a story, a lesson, and a unique emotion that shapes who we are. These encounters—some cherished, others challenging—remain with me, tucked into the corners of my memory, forming a collection of moments that define the journey of existence.

To my mother and father, whose love and unwavering support have been the foundation of my dreams and ambitions. My mother, a guiding light, and my father, a quiet force of strength. Though he has now moved on to his heavenly abode, his presence is as vivid as ever in my heart. He left just months before this book came to fruition, yet I feel his watchful eyes from above, his blessings cascading over me like an invisible embrace. Father, you are missed beyond words, but I carry your wisdom and grace in every step I take.

To my beloved wife, my steadfast companion, and my greatest cheerleader. Your selfless love is the cornerstone of my existence, the anchor that steadies me in the stormiest of seas. From the inception of this book to its very last page, you have been there—offering ideas, reviewing chapters, and refining my thoughts with a patience and devotion that leaves me in awe. Your anticipation for this book's completion was a constant reminder of why I write—to share stories that connect, inspire, and endure. You are my muse, my strength, and my greatest blessing.

This book is not just mine; it belongs to all of you. For the stories we've shared, the sacrifices you've made, and the love you've given unconditionally. This is a tribute to the moments we've lived and the memories we've created together. Thank you for being my reason, my inspiration, and my eternal source of strength.

"Beneath every brushstroke lies a secret, and behind every masterpiece, a story untold. Life, like art, is a canvas—its beauty revealed not just in its finished form, but in the scars, the colors, and the emotions that bring it to life."

Prelude

Art is often seen as a reflection of life—its triumphs, its tragedies, its intricate dance between hope and despair. But what happens when a single painting holds within its strokes the story of a life left unfinished, of love that lingers, and of dreams suspended in time?

The Unfinished Portrait is more than a tale of two lives intertwined by fate; it is a journey through the depths of human emotion, the pursuit of understanding, and the quiet beauty of moments that often go unnoticed.

From the bustling streets of Noida to the tranquil valleys of Kedarnath, this story unravels with every step Gaurav takes, driven by more than just professional ambition. It is a journey of discovery, one that seeks something far deeper—a connection, a revelation, a truth that lingers in the air like an unanswered prayer.

At its core, this tale explores how a fleeting encounter, a mere three days in the vast expanse of a lifetime, can profoundly alter the course of one's life. It is in those brief yet transformative moments with strangers that we often find answers to the questions we didn't even know we were asking. In the quiet resonance of shared silences and unexpected conversations, life offers us a glimpse of its intricate design, reminding us that every meeting holds the potential to reshape our understanding of the world—and ourselves.

This book is an ode to the serendipity of life, where chance meetings become life-altering, and the threads of destiny weave unexpected patterns. It celebrates perseverance, belief in fate, and the extraordinary narratives hidden in the folds of ordinary days.

As you turn these pages, immerse yourself in this journey. Feel the chill of the mountain air brushing against your skin, hear the echoes of untold tales in the whispering winds, and witness how a shared story between two strangers can illuminate the profound beauty of existence.

Some encounters are fleeting, yet they leave behind an indelible mark. Some questions linger unanswered until the moment we are ready to find them. Welcome to a story where three days—and a single brushstroke—change everything.

A Note from the Author

Writing this book was an emotional journey, one that transcends the act of mere storytelling. It began as an idea sparked by a conversation with friends, where we lamented the lack of heartfelt, genuine romance in modern movies. I decided then that I would write a romance that wasn't just a story, but an experience—one that would transport the reader into a world filled with love, emotions, and depth. My passion for painting also guided the narrative, as I wanted to create a world where art and emotions collided, blending color and feeling in a way that would evoke something real and authentic.

As with all creative endeavors, this book wasn't without its challenges. Life, with its twists and turns, often mirrored the journey of writing. Plotting the characters, especially giving them depth and direction, proved difficult at times. But nothing compared to the challenge of crafting the climax—a moment where every emotion and event had to come together in a way that felt both surprising and inevitable.

I must also admit that this story is deeply personal. There is a piece of me in every page. I met someone once, years ago, more than two decades and though I never knew her name, she left an indelible mark on my heart. That fleeting moment, that brief encounter, inspired the core of this story. It's a reminder that sometimes, a single connection, a single conversation, can change the course of your life.

To my readers, my message is simple: I hope you enjoy this story as much as I did writing it. It's a love story that's both conventional and modern, raw and tender. It's about the kind of love that isn't just about romance, but about the deeper connections we form with each other, and with ourselves. It's about the purity of love, and how it can change everything—if you're open to it.

Thank you for taking this journey with me.

With love,

Abhishek Bhatt

Contents

"In the silence between the brushstrokes, I found the echo of a love that could never be finished.

15th September

On that rainy day, I felt worried because I was already late for work. To make matters worse, my phone's battery was almost dead, heightening my sense of urgency. Without wasting any time, I grabbed my charger and hurried out the door, hoping against hope to catch the metro in time.

The city was a blur of drenched streets and honking vehicles, the rain adding a cinematic layer of drama to my rushed commute. By the time I reached the office, my clothes were slightly damp, and my heart was still racing. The familiar buzz of activity greeted me as I stepped inside. My eyes quickly scanned the room and landed on Rahul, my closest friend at work. He was lounging near the coffee machine, a warm smile playing on his face despite the dreary weather outside. I waved at him with a mix of nerves and excitement.

With a shaky smile, I approached him quietly and asked, "Hey, where's the boss?" My voice carried the weight of my anxiety.

Rahul, ever the calm one, gave me a reassuring shrug. "He hasn't shown up yet. Relax," he said with his trademark ease.

Waves of relief washed over me, and I let out a long, soothing exhale. Feeling lighter, I decided to treat myself to a comforting cup of coffee before heading to my cabin.

By the way, my name is Gaurav, and I'm 40 years old. I work at a dynamic advertising agency and media house called CommCreative. It's an exciting job where we brainstorm ideas, craft strategies, and bring advertising campaigns to life for our clients. It's a place where creativity thrives, and every day feels like a new challenge. Rahul and I, however, have a slightly different role here. We both work for the company's magazine division, which focuses on showcasing creative stories and compelling interviews. We met three years ago during our interviews, which, by sheer coincidence, were scheduled on the same day. We both got selected and even shared the same joining date. Since then, we've been an inseparable duo, tackling deadlines and sharing countless laughs along the way.

Our primary responsibility involves reviewing advertisements for the magazine and assisting journalists in crafting engaging interviews. It's a collaborative role, and I've grown to appreciate the blend of creativity and precision it demands. That morning, as I sipped my coffee, I sat at my table, minding my own business, when something caught my eye.

A magazine lay open right in front of me, its glossy pages practically inviting me to explore. Unable to resist, I picked it up and flipped to the first page. My breath hitched. There it was — a captivating picture of a blurred, half-finished portrait. The artwork was mesmerizing, its unfinished strokes exuding a sense of mystery and allure that was impossible to ignore.

My curiosity piqued, and without a second thought, I called out to Rahul. "You've got to see this!" I said, waving the magazine in the air.

Rahul sauntered over, intrigued by my excitement. The moment his eyes landed on the portrait; his brows lifted in surprise. Little did I know, that innocent moment of discovery would spark a conversation that would soon unravel into an endless thread of intrigue, excitement, and awe.

Rahul, with his trademark sarcastic tone, smirked and said, "Dude, let me tell you something mind-blowing about artists. These folks have this uncanny ability to create the most bizarre and out-of-this-world stuff, and guess what? People go absolutely nuts for it! They're ready to empty their wallets, throwing cash left and right just to get their hands on those paintings. It's like a frenzy out there! I mean, you won't believe it, but there are even bidding wars happening for these artworks. It's like a battle of the wallets! These artists have this magical power to capture something extraordinary and turn it into pure gold. It's crazy, man! Who knew that a splash of colors on a canvas could ignite such passion and obsession in people? The world of art is like a wild ride, and we're just lucky enough to witness it firsthand."

I raised an eyebrow and shot back with a grin, "Oh, brother! Whose consent has finally graced us today? Every single day, you unleash a barrage of curses upon celebrities. What's with the sudden fascination?"

Rahul chuckled, shaking his head. "Arrey yaar, look at this magazine. I'm talking about this guy—

Abhimanyu Chauhan. He makes very strange paintings. Anyway, I don't understand the art of any artist; their work is just too strange for me to really get."

"Yes," I nodded. "I've also heard he's an exceptional artist. But tell me, why are you abusing him?"

Rahul leaned against the desk, his tone more reflective now. "I'm not here to curse or insult anyone, my friend. But think about it for a moment. We slog away for 10-12 hours a day, and what do we get in return? A meager salary that barely covers our household expenses, with half of it vanishing into EMI payments. And then there are these artists who create something out of seemingly crooked lines on a piece of paper, and people marvel at their paintings as if witnessing wonders of the world."

He gestured dramatically, mimicking an art critic. "No one truly comprehends it all, yet they discuss amongst themselves as if they're art experts, as if they possess the wisdom of Picasso himself.

'Jis gehraayi se yeh banaya gaya hai woh saaf nazar aata hai painting mein.'

'Yeah, you're right, I can relate to this. I mean, just see the deep thought behind this.' Blah blah blah."

I laughed, shaking my head at his animated impression. "Alright, alright. I get it. But there must be something remarkable about their work if it can draw so much attention and admiration."

Rahul shrugged. "Maybe. Or maybe it's just a big scam. Who knows? Either way, people seem to love it."

I leaned back slightly, trying to calm the tension. "It's okay, bro, relax. Whatever is being discussed, there are clearly people out there who admire him and his art deeply. If he's famous today, he must have put in an incredible amount of effort to get where he is. Otherwise, wouldn't everyone just become a painter?"

Rahul rolled his eyes in mock annoyance. "Oh great, here comes your daily dose of wisdom."

"Hey, wait a second," I said, raising my hand defensively. "I'm not lecturing you. I'm just saying, think about it. If this guy's name is on everyone's lips and we're sitting here discussing him, there has to be something extraordinary about him, right? Ordinary people don't get this kind of attention." I picked up the newspaper from the desk and pointed at an advertisement. "Just look at this ad for his upcoming exhibition. The design is absolutely brilliant."

Rahul's curiosity piqued as he took the paper from me. His eyes lit up as he scanned the details. "You won't believe it, but when I saw this ad earlier, I couldn't look away. It's for Abhimanyu's exhibition, happening right here in the city in just three weeks. And what caught my eye?" He leaned closer, gesturing at the image. "It's a half-finished face, deliberately blurred, with the caption 'Hope to complete it soon.' Genius, right? The design is so captivating and original; it's impossible not to be impressed."

"Exactly!" I said, leaning forward with enthusiasm. "It's human nature to crave more when we're given less. Think of movie trailers. They only reveal enough to intrigue us, but it's enough to make us want to see the whole film. And artists like Abhimanyu? They're masters of this art of curiosity. They know how to draw you in and leave you wanting more."

Rahul chuckled, standing up. "Well, all this deep talk about art has left me craving something else. Let's go grab a cigarette."

"Yeah, and coffee too," I added with a smile as I got up to join him. "If the boss decides to call a meeting, we'll need all the energy we can get."

Rahul glanced at me as we sipped our coffees. "By the way, tell me, what do you think about this Abhimanyu? Is he really talented or just overhyped? I mean, you're an artist too. You could probably pull this off if you tried."

I laughed, shaking my head. "Oh, come on! We barely have time to breathe, let alone indulge in art. But, funny enough, I've heard his name before. My cousin, who's studying arts and painting in London, mentioned him once. Apparently, Abhimanyu visited their college. Small world, right?"

"Oh, seriously? He's that famous?" Rahul asked, raising an eyebrow.

"You have no idea," I replied with a grin. "My cousin was gushing about him, saying he's practically worshipped in the art world. People don't just admire him; they idolize him."

Before we could dive deeper into our conversation, my phone buzzed. It was my boss. His tone was brisk as he asked me to come to his office immediately. My heart skipped a beat as I hurried to his door, curiosity and nerves battling within me.

As I stepped inside, he wasted no time getting to the point. "I've got something interesting for you," he said. "I want you to assist one of our journalists with an interview… with Abhimanyu Chauhan."

For a moment, I was speechless. Meeting Abhimanyu Chauhan? The artist everyone was raving about? My mind raced with thoughts. That unfinished portrait flashed in my head, and the words "Hope to complete it soon" resonated deeply. There had to be a story behind it, and I was determined to uncover it.

Gathering my courage, I spoke up. "Boss, can I… can I take this interview myself?"

He looked at me, clearly surprised. "Aaj yeh interview lene ka shauk kaise chad gaya?"

I took a deep breath and replied earnestly, "I don't know, but I feel like I should do this. I want to."

He studied me for a moment, then nodded. "Okay. But if anything goes wrong, it's on you. I trust you won't let me down."

Now that I had asked my boss for permission and received his approval, I couldn't shake the nervousness deep inside me. There was a mountain of preparation to be done, and the weight of it settled on my shoulders.

My boss must have sensed my unease, because he gave me a reassuring pat on the back. "Don't worry, Gaurav. You've got this," he said with a smile. "Abhimanyu is a genuinely amiable person, and I'm confident he'll be more than happy to chat with you."

His words, though comforting, didn't completely ease my nerves, but they did spark something in me—determination. I was genuinely intrigued about meeting Abhimanyu, about understanding how his brilliant mind worked, and uncovering the inspiration behind his art.

As I stepped out of the office, a wave of excitement slowly began to replace my anxiety. The thought of meeting Abhimanyu Chauhan—the artist whose work had captivated the world—stirred a cocktail of emotions inside me: joy, curiosity, and a bit of bewilderment. It was hard to wrap my mind around the fact that I was going to have the opportunity to speak with him.

I couldn’t wait to delve into the depths of his creative process, to learn from his experiences, to unravel the mysteries that fueled his artistic genius. A sense of eagerness began to burn within me.

Despite my excitement, I knew that what lay ahead wouldn't be easy. I hadn’t interviewed someone of Abhimanyu’s stature before, and that thought sent a ripple of anxiety through me. I needed someone to talk to, someone who could calm my nerves. And Rahul, my trusted confidant, was always the person I turned to for guidance.

I made my way to Rahul, my mind still swirling with the weight of the task ahead. As soon as I told him the news, I saw the change in his expression—a moment of confusion, followed by a flicker of amusement. He was silent for a few seconds, processing what I had just shared, and I could see him trying to make sense of the situation.

But then, Rahul couldn't hold back his laughter, and I instantly knew I was in for some playful teasing. "Bro, this is KISMAT!" he exclaimed, still chuckling. "Just now we were discussing about him? Well, now you're the one who's got to interview one. Looks like it's promotion time!"

Despite the flush of embarrassment creeping up my neck, I couldn't help but join him in laughter. We joked and teased each other, laughing about the irony of the situation. I felt a lightness I hadn't expected—having Rahul's humour to lean on made the pressure of the moment a bit easier to bear. I knew, no matter how much I stumbled through this experience, he'd be there to support me. That knowledge brought a sense of comfort and reassurance I hadn't realized I needed.

We made our way downstairs, grabbing chai and cigarettes, all the while continuing our banter and marveling at how life seemed to throw these curveballs. Even though I was still anxious about the interview, the thought of Rahul by my side kept me grounded. It reminded me that I wasn't alone in this, and that made all the difference.

In the days that followed, I threw myself into researching Abhimanyu's life and his remarkable artistic journey. I became fully absorbed in learning about him, leaving no detail uncovered. Every nugget of information I found, I scribbled down in my notebook, poring over each one with careful attention. I wanted to understand him—not just as an artist, but as a person—before I even met him.

But preparation wasn't limited to research. I spent countless hours practicing my interviewing skills, refining my ability to ask insightful, thoughtful questions. I crafted a list of inquiries that I hoped would unlock the essence of his creativity, that would help me peel back the layers of his mind and reveal the driving force behind his art. The anticipation built inside me, and with each passing day, I felt a growing excitement. I was on the verge of an incredible opportunity—one I was determined to seize with both hands.

When my boss agreed to my request for the daunting task of interviewing Abhimanyu, I knew the weight of the responsibility I had just taken on. The importance of being fully prepared couldn't be overstated. Without wasting a single moment, I threw myself into research, eager to uncover every detail of his life and work. My mission was clear: to understand not just his artistic expressions, but the man behind them.

I plunged into a wealth of material—articles, interviews, speeches—every bit of information I could find about him. Each source became a stepping stone, offering me insights into his preferences, interests, and the essence of his art. I wanted to familiarize myself with his background and immerse myself in the unique style that defined him.

But I wasn't satisfied with simply skimming the surface. I wanted to make my interview with Abhimanyu something memorable. A conversation that would reveal not just his creative process, but the heart of his vision and the wellspring of his inspirations. To do that, I knew I had to ask questions that were different, questions that would offer our audience a rare glimpse into the depths of his mind.

I was determined to avoid the cliché, the repetitive questions he must have answered a thousand times. Instead, I sought to explore uncharted territory, to ask questions that would peel back the layers and expose new facets of his artistic journey. My goal was to create an interview that would be as enlightening for Abhimanyu as it would be for our audience.

The more I researched, the more I was captivated by the depth of Abhimanyu's connection to nature and culture. His art seemed to spring from a profound love for the world around him—breathtaking landscapes, towering mountains, lush jungles, and the vibrant spirit of Indian heritage. His creations spoke volumes about his reverence for the beauty that surrounded him.

I was also awestruck to learn how far his art had traveled. His exhibitions had crossed borders, showcasing his work in countries all over the globe. It was clear that his art transcended geographical and cultural boundaries, touching people from all walks of life and resonating with them on a deeply universal level.

This only fueled my determination to make our conversation something that would honor the power of his art.

As I meticulously took notes, I began crafting a list of questions that felt more like a map, guiding me toward the heart of Abhimanyu's artistic vision. I was eager to explore the origins of his creativity, to understand the spark that ignited the ideas behind his breathtaking paintings. Each question I shaped was designed to peel back the layers of his artistic soul, to reveal the thought process that breathed life into his masterpieces.

But as I dove deeper into my research, a fascinating discovery caught my attention—a hidden gem that only deepened my curiosity. It was a painting, one that seemed to hold a special place in Abhimanyu's heart. Unlike his celebrated landscapes or vibrant cultural depictions, this artwork was a captivating portrait.

What intrigued me even more was the fact that this particular piece had never been up for sale. It was a constant companion, accompanying him to every exhibition, as if it were a silent testament to something far more personal than any of his other works. The fact that this portrait existed amidst a body of work dominated by sweeping landscapes and cultural imagery sparked a fire of curiosity inside me. I became determined to uncover the story behind this enigmatic masterpiece.

I longed to understand the emotions behind it, the meaning that lay hidden beneath the surface. What was it about this painting that caused Abhimanyu to keep it so close, to never let it leave his side? The contrast it created within his artistic portfolio only deepened the mystery. The idea that this portrait held a secret, an untold story, became an irresistible puzzle I was determined to solve.

To my astonishment, I discovered that Abhimanyu had been questioned about this very painting on several occasions. International journalists had tried, unsuccessfully, to unlock its secrets, only to be met with vague, evasive answers. This only added to the enigma, pushing me further into my quest. The mystery of this painting was now personal—it was no longer just about uncovering a story, but about uncovering a part of Abhimanyu himself.

The fact that he had carefully guarded this secret gave the whole situation an exhilarating twist. It made me even more determined to be the one who finally unlocked the story behind the painting. The idea that I could be the one to coax Abhimanyu into sharing the emotions and insights concealed within that artwork was both thrilling and humbling. This was no longer just an interview; it was an opportunity to touch something deeply personal and intimate.

I decided to approach the interview with Abhimanyu meticulously, crafting a list of unique questions after delving into thorough research. I wanted to learn about his inspirations, his creative process, and, of course, the story behind the portrait that had captivated my curiosity. I hoped my preparation would impress him and make him more open to sharing his thoughts.

As I continued my research, a delightful discovery caught me by surprise. Abhimanyu, it turned out, had a passion for poetry and singing. Although he wasn't one for parties, he found joy in karaoke and wouldn't hesitate to join in if there was one nearby and he had the time. This revelation fascinated me, especially since most people only knew him for his art. I couldn't help but wonder how his love for poetry and music might influence his paintings. Perhaps these creative outlets intertwined, shaping the themes in his artwork. I made a mental note to bring this up during the interview, hoping it would offer deeper insight into his personality and artistic style.

"Not all love stories are meant to end. Some are simply meant to be remembered."

25th September

With only ten days remaining until the exhibition, I felt the pressure building. Time was slipping away, and I had so much to organize for the interview. I realized I needed to act fast. Summoning my courage, I reached out to the venue partner, hoping they could provide me with Abhimanyu's contact details and let me know when he would be arriving in the city. However, my request was met with resistance. They refused to share any information, and I could feel my frustration growing.

Unsure of what to do next, I decided to seek help from the event organizers. One of the staff members, fortunately, turned out to be incredibly kind and understanding. They empathized with my situation and suggested I contact Abhimanyu's team directly. It felt like a glimmer of hope in the midst of my struggle. Grateful for the advice, I quickly noted down the contact details for his manager and reached out without hesitation.

By some stroke of luck, I discovered that a friend of a friend was involved in the organizing team. It felt like a break after days of setbacks. Finally, after two relentless days of trying, I obtained the contact information for Abhimanyu's PR team. A wave of relief washed over me, and I couldn't help but feel a sense of triumph.

I contacted his PR team with a mix of excitement and anticipation, eagerly awaiting a response. Soon, I received the news I had been waiting for—Abhimanyu would be arriving in the city one week before the exhibition, just a day away. My heart raced as I mustered the courage to request a meeting with him. But the response I received left me in suspense: "We will let you know." The uncertainty gnawed at me, mixing hope with anxiety as I awaited their next move.

I couldn't help but feel a sense of disappointment. Despite my relentless efforts, I still hadn't managed to schedule a meeting with Abhimanyu. The uncertainty was wearing me down. Yet, amid the frustration, there was a flicker of hope, a tiny light that refused to be extinguished. Maybe, just maybe, there was still a chance to meet him after all.

Just when I was at my lowest, Rahul reached out. His voice was a balm for my weary soul. As I poured out my frustrations, he listened with the patience and understanding only a true friend can offer. Then, in his typical reassuring way, he said three words that meant the world to me: "Don't worry, you will get it." It was as though his belief in me became my own lifeline, pulling me from the brink of hopelessness and giving me a fresh surge of determination when I was ready to throw in the towel.

Finally, it was Friday—the day everyone looks forward to. As the evening drew near, Rahul suggested we meet up for some beers, a tradition we'd been keeping for as long as I could remember. After a long and exhausting week, it was the perfect way to unwind. I was eager for a change of pace, and I happily agreed. There was something comforting about the familiar routine of gathering with friends, sharing laughter, and simply forgetting the worries of the week.

Before I left, I called Neha, my wife, to let her know that I might be late for dinner. A twinge of sadness hit me because I knew we wouldn't get to enjoy our usual evening together. But as always, Neha's loving and understanding voice soothed me. She reminded me, with her quiet strength, that she would always support me—no matter how late I came home or how many obstacles I faced. Her unwavering belief in me was a steady anchor, giving me the courage to keep moving forward.

With a mix of emotions—hope, excitement, and a hint of guilt—I set out for the evening, ready to enjoy the company of my friends and take a break from the mounting pressure. The weekend held the promise of relaxation, and maybe, just maybe, the chance to find clarity amidst the chaos.

We were both in high spirits when we met at one of our favorite spots in Noida, a place where countless memories had been made and our friendship had deepened. Just stepping into that familiar environment filled us with a sense of excitement. As we sat down, the anticipation hung in the air—this was our space to relax, reflect, and share our thoughts. Naturally, our conversation turned to Abhimanyu Chauhan, and soon, he became the focal point of our discussion.

We threw around ideas and strategies for the interview, with Rahul injecting his usual humor, lightening the mood with funny quips that made us laugh and helped ease the weight of the task ahead. But underneath the laughter, a steady determination began to grow within me. While we joked and shared stories, my mind was racing in a different direction. I realized that if I only met Abhimanyu for the interview, he might not feel comfortable enough to truly open up. He had arrived a week ahead of the event, leaving me with a few days to establish a personal connection—a window of opportunity that felt both precious and fleeting. But how could I make that happen?

As we soaked in the cozy atmosphere, I found myself lost in thought. The more I mulled it over, the heavier the decision became. Should I take a chance and try to meet him outside the formal setting of the interview, to build some rapport? Or should I simply wait for the interview, letting it unfold naturally? The question lingered, and I couldn't shake the uncertainty that gripped me. Time seemed to slow down as I weighed my options.

A mix of emotions swirled inside me—curiosity, determination, and just a hint of nervousness. The idea of connecting with Abhimanyu on a more personal level consumed me. It wasn't just about the interview anymore; it was about understanding the man behind the artist, finding a way to unlock the thoughts and experiences that shaped his creative vision. This thought became an obsession, driving my every move and shaping the course of the days to come.

As I headed back home, my mind was a whirlpool of thoughts and emotions. It was late, nearly 11:30, and everything around me seemed unusually quiet, like the world had paused for a moment. When I reached the front door, I moved gently, careful not to disturb Neha, who was sound asleep inside. The peacefulness of her slumber made me feel tender and protective.

Inside, my thoughts were racing. I wanted to share everything with her—the excitement, the uncertainty, the hopes that filled me up—but I knew she had her own rhythm, her own routine. Neha had always been diligent about balancing her work and rest, and I couldn't bear the thought of waking her and disrupting the quiet harmony she had cultivated.

With a deep breath, I made the decision to wait until the morning. I promised myself I would share everything with her when the timing was right, when we could truly talk without the weight of exhaustion hanging over us.

To soothe my restless mind, I drank a glass of cool water. The crispness settled me, and for a moment, I felt the tension in my chest loosen. I was drained from the day's events—the constant push and pull of uncertainty—and from keeping my thoughts to myself. So, with a quiet surrender, I went to bed, hoping sleep would clear my mind and give me the clarity I needed for the next chapter of my journey.

The night wrapped its calm around me, and in that silence, I found solace. Tomorrow would bring a new day, a fresh start—and with it, the chance to share my thoughts with someone who always knew how to make everything seem a little bit clearer.

"A portrait is never truly complete. Like love, it lives in the spaces between what is seen and what is felt."

26th September

When the next day arrived, I could barely contain my excitement. I couldn't wait to tell Neha everything—the breakthrough I'd had with Abhimanyu's PR team, the hope of finally meeting him in person. But as I shared the news with her, I could sense the timing wasn't quite right.

Lately, Neha had been swept up in her own whirlwind of work. As a freelancer in digital marketing, collaborating with high-profile brands, she had built a career that demanded focus and energy. I couldn't help but admire her for it—her dedication, her drive, her ability to juggle everything with grace. Even when her schedule was packed, she never wavered in her support for me, inspiring me with her creativity and unique perspective. It was in moments like these that I felt even more grateful for her presence in my life.

Neha's brilliance went far beyond her work. She had a rare gift for infusing magic into the everyday. Whether she was helping our daughter, Samaira, with her schoolwork or simply managing daily routines, she had a way of turning even mundane tasks into engaging moments. Her knack for making life exciting was one of the many reasons I often sought her advice. She had a remarkable ability to cut through complexity, offering insights that were both practical and profound. Having her by my side felt like navigating life with a guiding light—steady, reassuring, and always illuminating the best path forward.

As the day unfolded, I found myself looking forward to sharing my updates with Neha. It struck me how deeply she had influenced my life—not just as my partner but as my inspiration, my anchor, and my unwavering source of support. She had a way of making every challenge seem surmountable, every problem solvable.

When we finally sat together at the breakfast table, I was eager to share my recent progress. But as I began, I noticed the telltale signs of a busy day ahead for her—a series of meetings already lined up in her calendar. I felt a pang of disappointment, but it was quickly overshadowed by her warmth. True to her nature, Neha didn't let her packed schedule diminish her care for us.

"Since you'll be home today," she said, her tone light and full of trust, "why don't you pick up Samaira from school? She'll be thrilled, and it's Saturday—your tradition."

Her request filled me with a sense of purpose. Our Saturday school pickups had become something special, a bond shared between father and daughter. Eagerly, I took on the role of being Samaira's protector and guide as she navigated the bustling school corridors.

The day passed in a flurry of activity—household chores, preparations, and the joy of picking up Samaira, who greeted me with her usual bright enthusiasm. By the time evening approached, I was settling into the rhythm of our day when Neha's call interrupted my thoughts. Her voice, as always, carried comfort.

"My meetings might run late tonight," she began, "but how about we go out for dinner? Just the three of us."

Her suggestion warmed my heart, a gentle reminder of the small joys that tethered us amidst our busy lives. I eagerly agreed, and soon, Samaira and I were ready to pick up Neha from her office, excitement sparkling in our daughter's eyes at the thought of an evening out.

We chose a cozy restaurant not far from home, a tranquil haven from the chaos of the city. In the soft glow of candlelight, I finally shared my news—the breakthrough with Abhimanyu's PR team, the looming possibility of an interview, and the exhaustive research I had undertaken to prepare. As I spoke, I saw Neha's eyes light up with genuine pride and curiosity.

"I want your help," I admitted, leaning into the moment. "Your perspective always brings clarity. I want to craft questions that aren't just insightful but will truly reveal who he is—the heart behind the art."

Neha smiled, her understanding palpable. She was always more than just a listener; she was a partner who elevated every endeavor, infusing it with her unique brilliance. In that moment, surrounded by warmth, love, and the promise of new possibilities, I felt a surge of gratitude for the life we had built—a life full of connection, inspiration, and unwavering support.

During our dinner, the warm aroma of spices and the mingling flavors of the food created a comforting atmosphere. As we talked, the conversation drifted to my dreams and ambitions, a subject that had always drawn us closer. Neha's eyes held a steady, unwavering belief in me—a quiet reassurance that reminded me of her steadfast presence in my life. In that moment, surrounded by her love and understanding, I felt invincible, as though together, we could conquer any challenge.

As the evening unfolded, there was a subtle mix of excitement and uncertainty. Neha, with her unique interests and occasional detachment from the world of arts and social spheres, approached the topic of my passion with a quiet curiosity. I, in turn, felt a flicker of nervousness. Would she connect with my journey, so different from her own? Yet, I trusted her insight and craved her perspective, no matter how outside her realm this topic might seem.

The soft notes of live music began to weave through the room, creating a cocoon of serenity. Then, as if the universe had been listening, the artist played the gentle melody of "Dil Ka Aalam Main Kya Bataun Tujhe" from *Aashiqui*. It was a song from the early days of our love—a tune I had often sung to Neha, each note carrying the unspoken promise of our growing bond.

The moment felt surreal, the music enveloping us in its tender embrace. Our eyes met, and in the quiet stillness of that melody, the years seemed to dissolve. We were transported back to a simpler time, where the only thing that mattered was the joy of being together.

The room faded away, leaving only us and the echoes of a love that had matured yet remained timeless.

The song acted like a key, unlocking memories we hadn't revisited in years. As it ended, the weight of my recent worries lifted, replaced by laughter and warmth. The atmosphere between us shifted entirely, as if the music had opened a door to our past. We reminisced about old stories, shared forgotten anecdotes, and celebrated the journey we had traveled together. Time slipped away unnoticed as we lost ourselves in the comfort of our shared history.

When the night finally drew to a close, we stepped out into the crisp night air, carrying the melodies with us. The drive home became a continuation of the evening's magic. The familiar road seemed to transform into a pathway through time, each landmark sparking another memory or moment we cherished. The car was filled with old Hindi classics playing softly in the background, adding to the nostalgic spell of the night.

The burdens of the past days—my anxieties about work, Neha's demanding schedule—seemed lighter, almost inconsequential. The music and the memories reminded us of the love that had been the anchor in our lives, a love that had grown stronger through every trial.

As we crossed the threshold of our home, the sense of connection lingered, warm and reassuring. I resolved to hold onto this feeling, to protect and nurture the moments that bound us together. Life's storms would come and go, but in the calm of our shared memories and enduring love, I found my refuge. That night, as the echoes of music and laughter faded into the quiet of our home, I promised myself to always treasure the little moments that gave our lives their richest meaning.

"You can wait for years for a moment to come back, but time will always tell you if it was meant to stay."

27th September

The next morning began with the soft, melodic voice of my daughter, Samaira, gently waking me up. Her cheerful presence was my favorite alarm clock, and as she announced that there was no school today, a smile crept across my face. It was a part of our cherished routine, one of those small but meaningful rituals that made life so special.

At the breakfast table, the warmth of our family's bond filled the air, mingling with the enticing aroma of freshly brewed coffee and the comforting sweetness of pancakes. Laughter echoed softly, a soundtrack to the simple joys of togetherness. Yet, amidst this serenity, a growing sense of responsibility quietly settled over me. The day ahead held significance—the much-anticipated call from Abhimanyu Chauhan's team loomed closer, bringing with it equal measures of excitement and pressure.

As the minutes ticked by, I immersed myself in preparations, my mind a whirlwind of research and ideas. Each question I crafted felt like a thread, weaving together the narrative I hoped to explore with the enigmatic artist. I envisioned peeling back the layers of his creativity, unraveling the mysteries behind his most captivating works, especially one painting that had seized my imagination.

In the midst of my focused preparations, Neha's familiar voice broke through, grounding me in the present. Her concern and genuine interest were evident, and as I looked up, I saw her supportive gaze—a steady anchor in the midst of my whirlwind thoughts. Feeling her warmth, I opened up about my anticipation and nervousness, sharing how deeply I wanted this opportunity to be transformative. I spoke of the painting that had captivated me, a piece that seemed to hold secrets waiting to be uncovered, and how I yearned to tell its story.

Neha listened intently, her empathy shining through. Her understanding smile and the comforting embrace that followed dissolved my anxieties, replacing them with a renewed sense of purpose. She reminded me of the passion that had brought me to this point, gently encouraging me to trust my instincts. "You've worked so hard for this," she said softly, her words a soothing balm. "Trust yourself—you have everything it takes to make this moment count."

Her unwavering belief in me felt like a quiet force, lifting me up and filling me with a new vigor. It was as though her confidence had reignited a spark within me, reminding me why I had chosen this path in the first place.

As the day progressed, the urgency of time made every passing moment precious. Yet, Neha's constant presence was a source of solace, a reminder that I was not alone in this journey. Her quiet acts of support and her steadfast faith in my abilities fortified me, infusing my preparations with a deeper sense of purpose.

In the safety of our home, surrounded by love, I found my resolve growing stronger. The dreams I had once cautiously nurtured now felt alive with newfound energy, fueled by Neha's encouragement and the inspiration I drew from my family. I felt ready—not only to seize this opportunity but to embrace the challenges that lay ahead with courage and determination.

This wasn't just about an interview anymore; it was about stepping into a moment that could shape the course of my future. And as I sat there, refining my questions and revisiting my goals, I realized I wasn't doing it alone. Neha's belief in me, Samaira's laughter, and the love we shared as a family were all woven into my journey, giving me the strength to keep moving forward.

As the day drew to a close, I found myself immersed in a whirlwind of thoughts. The past few days had been a rollercoaster of emotions, each moment a testament to how deeply I cared about this opportunity. Yet, as I lay in bed, a rare sense of calm began to settle over me.

That evening, Neha and I sat down together, driven by the shared anticipation of what lay ahead. The air in the room buzzed with a quiet intensity as we brainstormed questions for the interview. Each question we crafted was a delicate balance between Abhimanyu Chauhan's personal experiences and professional triumphs. But there was one question—a singular, elusive thought—that hovered just beyond our reach. It felt like a hidden gem, a question that could reveal a story yet untold, a glimpse into the artist's soul.

With furrowed brows and unwavering focus, we pressed on, combing through every available piece of information about Abhimanyu. We had examined his publicly known works, dissected his interviews, and even speculated on the fragments of his life that had trickled into the media. But the sense of discovery we craved remained just out of grasp, as though the real story lay hidden beneath layers we had yet to peel back.

And then, like the first rays of sunlight breaking through a cloudy sky, Neha's voice cut through the fog of uncertainty. "What if," she began, her tone thoughtful yet filled with quiet conviction, "you imagined yourself as him? Step into his world. Picture yourself standing before a painting that holds a secret—a story only you know. What question would you want someone to ask to uncover that story?"

Her words sparked a fire within me. It was such a simple idea, yet it felt profound, like a key turning in a long-forgotten lock. Closing my eyes, I allowed myself to slip into the world of Abhimanyu Chauhan. I imagined the vivid colors of his art, the intricate details that spoke volumes, and the emotions embedded within each brushstroke. I sought the unspoken narratives behind his creations, the silent truths only he could reveal.

As my thoughts deepened, the elusive question began to take shape in my mind. It wasn't just about technique or inspiration; it was about the heart of his art. What story had he poured into his work that had yet to be heard? What moment in his life had left an indelible mark on his canvas? Slowly but surely, the question crystallized—a blend of curiosity, empathy, and a desire to unveil the essence of his journey.

It was a question designed not just for the world's curiosity, but to connect with the artist himself, to touch a part of his soul that had remained hidden from view. In that moment, I felt a quiet triumph. Neha's insight had been the catalyst I needed, a reminder of the power of perspective and imagination. Together, we had unlocked a door that led to the heart of the mystery.

As I opened my eyes, I looked at Neha, who was watching me with a knowing smile. "I think we've found it," I said, my voice steady yet brimming with excitement. She nodded, her confidence in me as unwavering as ever. That night, as sleep began to claim me, I felt a sense of fulfillment I hadn't known in days. We had taken a step closer to uncovering a story that, perhaps, even Abhimanyu Chauhan was waiting to share.

While online research and gathering information about someone can provide valuable insights, it's a far cry from truly immersing oneself in their world and understanding their deepest emotions. As I delved deeper into the mystery surrounding Abhimanyu Chauhan's enigmatic painting, it became increasingly clear that this piece of art held a deeply personal story—perhaps tied to a significant event, an individual, or an unforgettable moment in his life. Despite countless journalists attempting to uncover the truth, Abhimanyu had always sidestepped the question, adding layers to the intrigue.

Interestingly, his evasion didn't seem deliberate. In one rare interview, he had even hinted at the possibility of revealing the story one day, a glimmer of vulnerability that sparked hope in me. Could my interview be the moment he finally chose to open up? The possibility ignited a sense of determination within me, propelling me forward with an optimistic resolve.

As I poured over records of Abhimanyu's past exhibitions and promotional campaigns, a fascinating detail emerged. The mysterious painting that captivated me had never been featured prominently in his earlier marketing materials. Yet, in his latest advertisement, it was showcased front and center, a stark departure from his usual practice. This decision felt deliberate, almost as if he was signaling a readiness to unveil the story that had remained untold for so long. My heart leaped at the thought—could this truly be the moment of revelation? Or was I letting my imagination run wild, weaving significance where none existed? Choosing hope over doubt, I trusted my instincts and allowed myself to embrace the possibility of a breakthrough.

Fueled by a mix of excitement and nervous energy, I prepared for the upcoming interview with meticulous care. Each moment spent immersing myself in Abhimanyu's previous works felt like a step closer to understanding his artistic essence. I studied every brushstroke, every subtle nuance, as though they could guide me to the emotions he had poured into his creations. My goal wasn't just to ask questions but to connect with him on a profound level, to experience his art through his eyes and heart.

***"Love isn't about perfection—
it's about the moments that
linger, even when everything
else fades away."***

28th September

The next day brought a heightened sense of anticipation. As we gathered in the office, the air buzzed with unspoken excitement. Rahul, ever the curious companion, leaned over and asked, "Has the appointment with Abhimanyu been confirmed?"

I hesitated for a moment before answering. "Not yet," I admitted, feeling the weight of my own anticipation. "I'm waiting for their call. Hopefully, it'll come before lunchtime. If not..." I trailed off, already resolved to act. "I'll follow up myself. I can't risk letting this slip through the cracks."

Rahul nodded, understanding the urgency behind my words. The decision to take matters into my own hands wasn't born out of impatience but necessity. This opportunity, this moment, felt too important to leave to chance. My resolve solidified further as I silently prepared for whatever lay ahead, determined to bridge the gap between mystery and revelation.

As the morning stretched on, the silence of my phone became increasingly unbearable. Each passing minute felt agonizingly slow, and I found myself glancing at the clock more often than I cared to admit. Lunchtime came and went, leaving me with a growing sense of unease. The call I had been so anxiously anticipating remained elusive. Should I risk appearing overly persistent by calling again, or should I trust their promise and wait? The question gnawed at me, and the indecision felt like an anchor dragging me down.

Eventually, I took a deep breath and dialed the number. On the other end, a calm and composed voice greeted me—it was Shivani from Abhimanyu's team. My anxiety spiked as I explained my query, hoping for a definitive answer. Shivani listened patiently, her tone professional yet kind, and assured me she would call back within thirty minutes with an update.

Those thirty minutes felt like an eternity. The clock's relentless ticking seemed to mock my anticipation, each second stretching endlessly. I tried to distract myself, but my mind kept circling back to the waiting phone. When the promised time passed without a word, my restlessness grew unbearable. Yet, I hesitated to call again, fearing that persistence might be misconstrued as desperation. Instead, I resolved to wait a little longer, clinging to the hope that my patience would soon be rewarded.

Nearly an hour and a half later, the phone finally rang. The sharp trill pierced the oppressive silence, and my heart leaped in response. With a mix of nervousness and cautious optimism, I answered, bracing myself for whatever news awaited me.

Shivani's voice came through, steady but tinged with the subtle hesitancy of someone delivering unwelcome news. "Mr. Chauhan is already in town," she began, "but his schedule is incredibly packed. While you're on the list, I can't guarantee an appointment."

Her words hit me like a punch to the gut. The hope I had been clinging to unraveled in an instant, replaced by a heavy wave of disappointment. The meticulously built anticipation, the hours of preparation, the nervous excitement—all of it felt like it had crumbled to ash. I managed to thank Shivani and end the call, but the emptiness that followed was deafening.

The weight of her words hung over me, casting a shadow on my once-bright aspirations. It was as if all the effort I had poured into this pursuit had been rendered meaningless. The fire of my enthusiasm was extinguished, leaving behind a cold void of uncertainty and doubt.

I sat in silence, grappling with the crushing reality of an opportunity slipping through my fingers. Yet, amidst the gloom, a quiet voice within me urged me not to give up just yet. Perhaps this was only a setback, not the end of the journey. For now, though, all I could do was sit with my disappointment and gather the strength to find a way forward.

As I processed the news, a new worry began to gnaw at my mind. How would I explain this to my boss? The thought of facing disappointment and the possibility of judgment weighed heavily on me, adding another layer of stress to an already challenging situation. Feeling overwhelmed and in need of solace, I reached out to Rahul, my steadfast friend and confidant.

We decided to meet at our favorite café, seeking comfort in the familiar routine of sharing a coffee and a cigarette. The café's warm ambiance and the inviting aroma of freshly brewed coffee provided a temporary escape from the storm brewing inside me. Sitting across from Rahul, amidst the haze of swirling smoke, I finally let the floodgates open. I poured out my frustrations and fears, my voice tinged with the vulnerability I rarely allowed myself to show.

Rahul, with his characteristic patience, listened intently, offering a sympathetic ear. Sometimes, in the face of disappointment, all we need is someone who truly understands—a friend who reminds us that we're not alone. In that cozy corner of the café, we found comfort in each other's presence. The weight of my anxieties eased slightly as we talked, the act of sharing transforming the overwhelming burden into something more manageable.

Even though my disappointment lingered, having Rahul by my side made a world of difference. He was usually the one to lighten tense moments with humor, but this time, he chose a different approach. He could see how much this opportunity meant to me and sensed how deeply the setback had affected me.

With a steady gaze, he said, "You're always the one who finds the silver lining, the one who stays positive no matter what. Now, you're starting to lose hope. But don't worry, my friend. I believe in you. You will succeed—I'm sure of it."

His words were simple, but they carried a sincerity that cut through the fog of doubt clouding my mind. In that moment, his unwavering belief in me felt like a ray of sunshine piercing through the gloom. It reignited a flicker of hope deep within, a reminder that setbacks are not the end—they are simply challenges waiting to be overcome.

As we sat there, sipping coffee and exchanging thoughts, I felt a renewed sense of determination building within me. Rahul's support wasn't just a comforting presence; it was a catalyst, pushing me to face my struggles head-on. By the time we left the café, I no longer felt alone in my fight. Instead, I carried with me the quiet reassurance that, with friends like Rahul, I had the strength to keep going.

As I trudged home from the office, a heavy cloud of despair settled over me. The uncertainty surrounding the interview weighed on my mind, filling me with a deep and lingering sadness. What would become of me if this opportunity slipped through my fingers? All those cherished dreams of interviewing a renowned artist, of uncovering the hidden stories behind their masterpieces, seemed to dissolve into the void of uncertainty.

This interview wasn't just another assignment—it was my shining beacon, a milestone I had envisioned as transformative for my career. It held the promise of setting me apart, elevating my professional journey, and unlocking new doors of opportunity. But now, that dream felt fragile, threatened by forces beyond my control. The thought of it slipping away pressed heavily on my chest, threatening to snuff out the hope I had so carefully nurtured.

As I neared home, the weight of my disappointment must have been etched across my face, despite my attempt to mask it. My wife, Neha, with her unerring intuition, immediately saw through my facade. She possessed a remarkable ability to read the emotions I tried so hard to hide. Her tender gaze met mine, radiating understanding without the need for words.

Inside the sanctuary of our home, emotions ran high. We shared our worries and hopes in the intimate language only love can create. Together, we resolved to face whatever came next, resilient in the knowledge that our bond was our greatest strength.

After dinner, as the house settled into a tranquil hush, I sought refuge on the terrace. I craved the bittersweet comfort of a cigarette, its tendrils of smoke curling into the cool night air like a physical manifestation of the emotions swirling within me. The stars above seemed indifferent to my struggles, their steady light a stark contrast to the turmoil in my heart.

When Samaira finally drifted off to sleep, Neha joined me on the terrace. She didn't speak immediately but stood beside me, her presence grounding. Finally, she broke the silence, her voice soft and concerned. She gently inquired about the outcome of my appointment, her tone revealing the depth of her care. She rarely saw me smoke at home, and my actions tonight spoke volumes about the gravity of the situation.

With a heavy heart, I shared the uncertain news I had received from Shivani. My words hung in the night air, heavy with disappointment and tinged with the fragile hope I still clung to. Neha listened, her expression reflecting both empathy and determination. In her presence, I felt seen, understood, and, for a fleeting moment, less alone.

As I exhaled another plume of smoke, a blend of trepidation and determination flickered in my eyes. In that shared moment, Neha and I became partners in resilience, silently vowing to face the uncertainty together. Her unwavering belief in me was like a lighthouse in the storm, a steady beam guiding me through the shadows of doubt. With her by my side, I felt fortified, ready to weather whatever lay ahead.

That night, as whispers of doubt mingled with the faint aroma of tobacco, I clung to the fragile threads of hope that tethered us to brighter tomorrows. Through the haze of uncertainty, our love became my anchor, grounding me amidst life's tumultuous tides. In the quiet sanctuary of our bond, we found strength—a shared resolve that, against all odds, we would navigate our way forward.

Neha's voice, soft and soothing, wrapped around me like a comforting embrace. Her words carried the weight of faith—faith in destiny, in divine timing, in the unseen forces that shape our lives. It felt as though her words were carried by an angel, easing the burden that had settled heavily on my heart. Her belief was infectious, sparking a faint yet vital light within me.

In that moment, a glimmer of hope pierced through the dense fog of my thoughts. Neha's steadfast conviction that the universe worked in mysterious but benevolent ways rekindled my optimism. If the moon of opportunity was indeed destined to rise, I realized, the universe would conspire to ensure it graced my path.

As I pondered the road ahead, my mind wandered to vivid imaginings of serendipity. I allowed myself to dream of chance encounters and miraculous moments, where fate would intervene to connect me with Abhimanyu Chauhan. In those fleeting thoughts, I could almost picture a cinematic scene: two strangers crossing paths, transformed by a spark of destiny into allies on a shared journey.

Lost in these hopeful musings, I felt the weight of the day lift. The allure of sleep beckoned, and I surrendered, drifting into a realm where dreams blurred the edges of reality. In that space, my mind painted vivid scenes of fortuitous meetings and miraculous resolutions, offering solace in the boundless possibilities of the unknown.

As I slept, the burdens of the waking world dissolved into weightlessness, replaced by a sense of wonder and anticipation. Within the embrace of dreams, hope took flight, free from the constraints of doubt. It was there, in that ethereal landscape, that I found the strength to believe once more—in possibility, in destiny, and in the magic that shapes our lives in the most unexpected ways.

"Destiny doesn't always give us what we want. But sometimes, it gives us what we need, even if it's just the memory of a moment."

29th September

Next morning as I sat down for breakfast, absentmindedly flipping through the channels, a news bulletin caught my attention. The anchor's voice filled the room, announcing that the sacred Kedarnath Dham would soon close its gates on the 17th of October. Suddenly, my eyes widened with a glimmer of realization.

In that moment, a surge of excitement coursed through my veins as I connected the dots. Abhimanyu, the very person I had yearned to interview, was a devout follower of Lord Shiva. Every year, without fail, he embarked on a pilgrimage to the revered Kedarnath Dham. My heart skipped a beat as the significance of this discovery sank in.

Although Kedarnath Dham opened its doors to devotees for only six months, Abhimanyu had been away from the country for the past few months. This knowledge, thanks to the omnipresence of social media, had slipped into my grasp. In this digital age, one could uncover the whereabouts and activities of others, provided they chose to share them.

Gratitude washed over me, knowing that I had stumbled upon this vital information. I considered myself fortunate to have gained insights into

Abhimanyu's recent endeavors, exhibitions, guest lectures, and even his interviews. The power of technology had granted me a glimpse into his life, weaving a thread of connection between us.

The pieces of the puzzle began to align, painting a picture of possibility. The proximity of time and location offered a glimmer of hope, a chance to cross paths with Abhimanyu and unravel the layers of his enigmatic persona. As I savored my breakfast, the anticipation of what lay ahead tingled in the air, fueling my determination to seize this golden opportunity.

As the realization sank in that Abhimanyu was now in Delhi, my heart fluttered with a glimmer of hope. The synchronicity of the news bulletin and his presence in the city seemed more than mere coincidence. Could it be a divine sign, a message from the heavens above? Sitting there, contemplative and filled with anticipation, I pondered the possibilities that lay before me.

Instead of passively waiting for a miracle to transpire or for his call to come, I resolved to take matters into my own hands. Perhaps it was time to step out of my comfort zone and embark on a journey of my own making. After all, in this age of technological marvels, staying updated on the latest news and updates could be easily accomplished through a phone call.

I must confess, the desire to visit Kedarnath Dham had long been nestled in the recesses of my heart. However, circumstances had never aligned to grant me that cherished opportunity. It was often said by the elders that one can only have darshan of God when it is divinely ordained. In that moment, I couldn't help but perceive it as a call from the divine, a beckoning to seize the chance before me.

The prospect of venturing towards Kedarnath Dham now felt like a manifestation of destiny itself. With a newfound sense of purpose and determination, I resolved to follow the path that seemed to be unfolding before me. The longing within me, intertwined with a deep-rooted belief in the workings of a higher power, propelled me forward.

With hope kindled in my heart, I prepared myself for the journey that held the promise of both professional and personal fulfillment. A sense of awe and reverence filled my being as I contemplated the possibilities that awaited me on this sacred pilgrimage. Trusting in the divine guidance that had brought me to this moment, I took my first step towards Kedarnath Dham, ready to embrace the transformative power of faith.

With a sense of urgency, I turned to Neha and declared that we would be heading to Kedarnath Dham the very next day. Perplexed, she questioned the suddenness of the plan, sharing the weight of her responsibilities and the impending conference she couldn't afford to miss. Neha explained that visiting such places required careful preparation due to the cold climate, frequent rainfalls, and the possibility of snowfall. It wasn't as simple as picking up a few essentials and leaving on a whim. Moreover, Samaira's semester exams were just around the corner, necessitating leave from school.

Undeterred, I responded with a resolute determination. "I just feel the need to go," I asserted. Even if Neha couldn't join me, I was prepared to embark on this pilgrimage alone. There was an inexplicable pull within me, a belief that it was through this journey that God would guide me.

Though a tinge of anger colored Neha's expression, she acquiesced, recognizing the sanctity of the destination. "You are venturing to a place of God," she mused. "That's why I won't hold you back. If it were any other place, I would never let you go," she added, her words softened by a gentle laughter.

In that moment, a mix of emotions swirled within me. Gratitude washed over me for Neha's understanding, despite her reservations. Her unwavering support in acknowledging the significance of this spiritual endeavor touched my heart deeply. It was a testament to the depth of our bond and the acceptance of each other's journeys, even when they diverged.

The path to Kedarnath Dham beckoned, calling me to venture forth in search of solace and spiritual guidance. With Neha's reluctant blessing, I set forth on a voyage that held the promise of divine intervention, knowing that the love and support of my partner would always be with me, even in the face of uncertainty.

I scrambled to pack everything in such a short notice, feeling overwhelmed by the task at hand. Emotions were running high as I contemplated how to approach my boss for time off. With no opportunity to fix an appointment, the mere thought of requesting leave left me puzzled and anxious.

The following day, as I arrived at the office, my first instinct was to inquire about the boss's presence. I turned to Rahul, hoping for some clarity. He informed me that the boss hadn't arrived yet, but I couldn't shake off the unease that lingered within me. A phone call had come through earlier, and from the tone of voice, I sensed that boss was in a foul mood.

Caught in the grip of this predicament, my distress was evident on my face. Sensing my unease, Rahul approached me, concern etched on his features. He gently asked, "What's the matter? Why do you seem upset? Did you receive some updates? Did you manage to secure an interview?" My response was tinged with a mix of uncertainty. "I'll get to that, but right now, I'm worried about something else. I need to go somewhere urgently for 2-3 days, and considering the boss's foul mood, I'm at a loss for words when it comes to asking for leave."

As the weight of my circumstances settled upon me, I felt a surge of emotions welling up inside. The fear of facing an already disgruntled boss intensified my anxiety, making it difficult to articulate my needs. The uncertainty of how my request would be received gnawed at my conscience, as I desperately sought a solution to this emotional ordeal.

After what felt like an eternity, the boss finally arrived, and I seized the opportunity to make my way to his cabin. As I stood before him, anxiety gripped me, unsure of how he would react. His first question pierced the air, demanding an update on the interview preparations. Trying to maintain composure, I responded, "I'm on it, everything's going well." But in the depths of my being, nerves and doubts were bubbling, threatening to overshadow my words.

Summoning all my courage, I mustered the strength to broach the subject of my personal work, which required me to be away for 2-3 days. With hesitant words, I approached the topic, fully aware of the risk involved. The boss, engrossed in his laptop, continued his work without casting a glance at me. In a detached tone, he inquired if I wanted leave. My heart pounded with trepidation as I replied, "Yes, sir. Please don't worry. I'll try my best to complete your tasks." His response, though distant, carried a glimmer of acknowledgment. "I know you take your work seriously, and I trust that you will excel. However, time is of the essence, and I hope you realize the significance of this endeavor, both for yourself and our company." My voice trembled slightly as I assured him, "Sir, I will do everything in my power to meet and exceed your expectations."

Exhaling a sigh of relief, I felt a weight lift off my shoulders. At least one worry had been alleviated, and a flicker of hope ignited within me. The anticipation to leave and embark on my personal task grew with each passing moment. Evening arrived, and on my way home, I made sure to collect essential items, conscious of the impending early morning departure.

Upon reaching home, Neha, my dear companion, greeted me with warmth and care. Sensing my exhaustion, she informed me, "I've packed your belongings. Take a look to ensure nothing is left behind." Deep down, I knew that Neha had meticulously organized everything, sparing me the need to double-check. Overwhelmed by her thoughtfulness, I expressed my gratitude and retreated to bed early after dinner, knowing that a 4:00 am departure awaited me in the morning.

As I lay there, the emotions within me swirled—a blend of anticipation, nervousness, and a tinge of excitement for the journey ahead. Sleep eluded me momentarily, as my mind wandered through the possibilities and challenges that awaited me in the days to come.

"An unfinished portrait is a love story left incomplete, but maybe that's the most beautiful way to remember it."

30th September

As the morning light prepared to embrace the world, gently dispelling the darkness, I embarked on my journey, brimming with excitement and anticipation. The prospect of meeting Abhimanyu filled me with joy, and the fact that I was about to embark on my first trip to Kedarnath amplified my happiness. Determined to reach my destination on time, I had decided to undertake the adventure of self-driving, relishing the freedom it offered.

By 8:30 am, I found myself in Rishikesh, a serene haven. Fatigue started to creep in, and I realized that taking a moment to rest and savor a hearty breakfast would be wise. So, I paused to nourish both my body and soul. With renewed energy and a satisfied stomach, I resumed my journey at 9:00 am. The road ahead stretched through Devprayag, Srinagar, and Rudraprayag, each destination unfolding before my eyes like chapters in a mesmerizing tale.

The hilly terrain demanded caution, and I moderated my speed accordingly. Despite the well-maintained roads, my senses were heightened, mindful of every twist and turn. The clock struck 3 pm, and the realization dawned upon me that another break at this point might hinder my progress. Resisting the temptation to pause for a longer period, I settled for a cup of tea, a quick refresher to invigorate my senses. The urgency to reach Phata as swiftly as possible lingered in my mind, for there awaited the helicopter that would transport me to Kedarnath. Time was a precious commodity, and traversing the distance on foot would consume far too much of it.

With renewed determination, I set forth on the road once again. The engine hummed, and my focus sharpened as I navigated the winding path. Emotions tugged at my heartstrings as the rugged beauty of the landscape unfolded before me. Each passing moment brought me closer to my destination, and the anticipation grew with every mile covered. The thought of reaching Kedarnath, a place of spiritual significance, propelled me forward, overshadowing any weariness or obstacles that lay in my path.

As the sun began its descent, casting a warm golden glow over the mountains, I pressed on. The journey was arduous, but the fervor within me refused to waver. I held onto the belief that this expedition would be an experience to cherish, a testament to my determination and unwavering spirit.

As I ascended higher, the weather took a turn for the worse. Dark clouds loomed overhead, casting an ominous shadow on my journey. Undeterred, I sought solace in chanting Lord Shiva's bhajans, hoping for divine guidance and protection. Each verse uttered carried a flicker of hope amidst the challenging conditions.

By the time I reached Guptkashi, the clock struck 5:00 pm, and to my dismay, I encountered a sea of vehicles. The traffic congestion hindered my progress, prolonging the exhaustion that had settled within me. The reason became apparent—road widening work was underway, causing delays and frustration. Another hour crawled by before I finally arrived at the city's designated parking lot in Phata. Weariness clung to every fiber of my being as I stepped out of the car, my patience wearing thin.

Determined to salvage the situation, I made my way toward the helipad, a glimmer of hope igniting within me. However, reality struck me with a heavy blow. The weather conditions above were unforgiving, rendering the helicopter rides impossible for the time being. The authorities, considering safety paramount, had suspended operations until the following morning, contingent upon clear skies. The news hit me like a tidal wave, triggering a whirlwind of emotions. Frustration coursed through my veins, mingling with the weariness accumulated from the day's journey. The culmination of exhaustion and the proximity to my destination amplified this setback, exacerbating my anguish.

The inner turmoil intensified as I grappled with disappointment and anger. Fatigue and the sense of being so close to my goal only to face this obstacle heightened the emotional turmoil within me. Doubts crept in, questioning the validity of my efforts and the fairness of the situation. I yearned for a reprieve, a stroke of luck that would allow me to proceed with my pilgrimage as planned. The weight of the day's hardships and the additional setback loomed heavy on my spirit, challenging my resilience.

Yet, deep within me, a glimmer of hope persisted. I reminded myself that challenges are an integral part of any journey, and this setback would ultimately make the achievement all the more meaningful. With a heavy heart and a determination to persevere, I sought temporary refuge to gather strength for the uncertainties that awaited me on the horizon.

The very thought of embarking on a strenuous uphill climb on foot had filled me with apprehension. Yet, circumstances had led me to this point where there seemed to be no other viable option. Staying idle at the helipad all night felt like an utter waste of precious time, so I made the resolute decision to embrace the path of trekking. The car was already parked, so I embarked on a local jeep journey from Phata to Gaurikund, the starting point of the arduous trek.

As the jeep rumbled along the winding roads, doubts and uncertainties swirled within me. Would it be safe to trek at night? Such concerns plagued my mind. However, to my astonishment, I discovered that I was not alone in this endeavor. Numerous fellow pilgrims, hailing from different walks of life, shared the same determination. Among them was a spirited family from Delhi, with whom I had struck up a conversation during our journey from Phata in a fellow jeep. Their presence brought a comforting sense of camaraderie, dispelling some of my initial reservations.

Together, we set out on the challenging trail. Darkness engulfed our surroundings, intensifying the chill in the air. The biting cold penetrated through our layers of clothing, reminding us of the demanding conditions we willingly embraced. Raindrops occasionally cascaded upon us, adding to the already formidable test we faced. Fatigue started to set in, burdening my weary limbs. Recognizing my limitations, I made a pivotal decision at Garud Chatti. It was 3:00 am, and the combination of exhaustion, freezing temperatures, and the downpour compelled me to seek respite and rest.

The sheltered haven of Garud Chatti beckoned, offering solace amidst the formidable journey. With each passing moment, the significance of this pause grew, allowing me to gather my strength and rejuvenate my weary spirit. The decision to halt momentarily was not one of defeat but rather an act of self-preservation, acknowledging my physical and emotional limitations. Surrounded by the encompassing darkness and the symphony of raindrops.

I lacked the courage to continue walking, so I decided to take a much-needed rest for 2-4 hours. Setting my alarm for 6:00 in the morning, I eagerly sought solace in sleep.

"Some hearts are meant to be portraits, not to be held but to be admired from a distance, forever incomplete."

1st October

As I opened my eyes the next day, a breathtaking sight awaited me. The mountains were covered in a pristine layer of snow, as if a master artist had meticulously painted them in shades of white. It was a sight I had never witnessed before, and it stirred something deep within me.

Filled with awe and wonder, I resumed my journey after sipping a warm cup of tea. The picturesque views that surrounded me seemed like a surreal dream. I was captivated by the beauty that had eluded me during the previous night. The only sound echoing through the mountains was the rhythmic chant of "Har Har Mahadev, Jai Shiv Shambhu." In that moment, I experienced a spiritual awakening like never before. Emotions swelled within me, as if the divine presence was guiding me forward.

After walking for about an hour, the road gradually became flat. And there it stood, in all its glory, the majestic Kedarnath ji temple. A surge of electricity ran through my body, and I was overcome with goosebumps. It felt as if God Himself had bestowed His blessings upon me. In that instant, all the weariness and trials I had endured vanished into thin air. Tears welled up in my eyes, and I could feel a profound sense of gratitude washing over me.

I approached the temple with a mixture of reverence and humility. Each step I took felt like a step towards inner transformation. As I entered the hallowed grounds, the weight of the world seemed to lift from my shoulders. It was as if my burdens had been cast away, replaced by a deep sense of peace and tranquility. In that sacred space, I poured my heart out, offering my prayers and hopes to the divine.

This journey had become more than just a physical pilgrimage. It had become a pilgrimage of the soul. The emotional rollercoaster I had experienced along the way had transformed me from within. The challenges and doubts that had plagued me earlier had now been replaced by a newfound strength and resilience.

The moment I arrived at the destination, my heart skipped a beat. The place was swarming with tourists, bustling with energy and excitement. Finding a hotel seemed like an impossible task amidst the chaos. With each passing moment, my hopes of a comfortable resting place dwindled, and exhaustion started to creep in.

Finally, after what felt like an eternity, I stumbled upon a quaint hotel tucked away in a corner. Relief washed over me as I entered the premises, eager to freshen up and rejuvenate my tired soul. The warm water cascading down my body provided solace, washing away the weariness of the journey.

Once ready, I embarked on a spiritual quest to visit the sacred temple. Gratitude filled my heart as I stepped inside, for it was here that I could express my deepest gratitude to the divine. Amidst the throngs of devotees,

I sought solace and a chance encounter with Abhimanyu, whose presence held the key to my desires.

Lost in the sea of faces, I wondered how I would ever find him amidst this multitude. Desperation consumed me as I yearned for a sign, a guiding light to lead me to him. It was then that a kind soul, perhaps an angel in disguise, directed me towards a temple nestled high above – the abode of Bhairav Nath. They whispered, "If you seek his blessings, your journey will be complete, and your prayers shall be answered."

With a renewed sense of purpose, I ascended the hill, step by step, eager to catch a glimpse of the revered Bhairav Nath. As I climbed higher, the breathtaking vista of the Kedarnath valley unfolded before my eyes. Words failed me as I beheld the ethereal beauty that surrounded me. It was as if I had entered a realm of dreams, where nature's grandeur embraced my weary soul, offering respite from the burdens of everyday life.

Each footfall brought me closer to my destination, fueling a mix of anticipation and trepidation within me. The air grew crisp, carrying a subtle fragrance of incense and devotion. Emotions swirled in my chest, like a symphony of hope and uncertainty. The path ahead was steep, challenging my resolve, yet the allure of fulfillment kept me going.

Finally, I reached the summit, where the temple stood majestically. Time seemed to stand still as I approached the sacred abode. The atmosphere hummed with reverence, filling me with a deep sense of awe and reverence. Every step felt like a pilgrimage, a profound journey within myself.

I paid my respects and decided to sit for a while to absorb the tranquility of the place. The stillness around me was profound, offering a sense of calm I hadn't felt in days. Inspired by the serenity, I retrieved a diary and pencil from my bag and began sketching. From where I sat, the Kedarnath temple stood out beautifully, its grandeur magnified against the humble backdrop of the valley.

Engrossed in my sketch, I suddenly heard a voice from behind me, "You're very talented at sketching." Startled, I turned around and murmured a polite, "Thank you." But as my eyes met the speaker, I froze. It was him. The voice belonged to none other than Abhimanyu Chauhan himself.

In that instant, it felt as though my prayers had been answered almost too quickly, leaving me both thrilled and nervous. Struggling to process the moment, I fumbled, "Oh, what are you saying? This is nothing compared to your work. I only do this as a hobby."

Intrigued, Abhimanyu asked, "Do you know me?" For a fleeting moment, I considered feigning ignorance. But no matter how much I tried, I couldn't bring myself to lie. I nodded and replied, "Yes, I do. You're Abhimanyu Chauhan, right?" I extended my hand, which he shook warmly.

"How do you know me?" he asked, his curiosity piqued.

I hesitated, but honesty seemed the only path forward. "My name is Gaurav," I began. "I work for a media company in Noida. To be honest, I didn't know much about you until recently. A few days ago, I was assigned to cover your upcoming exhibition in Delhi, and I've been trying to secure an interview with you ever since. When all my attempts failed, I came here with a prayer to meet you, and now, I can't believe I'm actually sitting here, talking to you."

His expression shifted slightly, likely surprised to encounter a journalist in such an unexpected setting. Then, with a hearty laugh, he said, "You're very lucky. People wait for years for their prayers to be answered." His laughter broke the tension, and we began to talk.

We spent what felt like hours discussing everything under the sun—simple, everyday things. He even sketched a quick portrait of me. For a while, it felt less like a meeting between a journalist and an artist, and more like two strangers finding common ground. I refrained from bringing up the interview directly, careful not to disrupt the easy camaraderie we had found. Perhaps that's why he remained so relaxed, sharing bits of his thoughts and musings with me freely.

As the weather began to turn, clouds gathering ominously above us, we decided it was time to descend. We made our way back towards the hotel, the conversations lingering in the air like the fading light of the evening. I couldn't help but marvel at the serendipity of it all—how life sometimes delivers the most unexpected gifts, wrapped in the most unassuming moments.

The journey to the hotel was filled with a blend of emotions. A sense of gratitude overwhelmed me as I reflected upon the unexpected turn of events. The universe had conspired to bring us together, forging a connection that transcended professional boundaries. It was a testament to the power of genuine human interaction, the magic that can unfold when two souls intertwine.

A remarkable bond had formed between us within such a short span of time. As we began our descent, Abhimanyu inquired about my place of stay. I confessed that my visit had been unplanned, resulting in my choice of a hotel near the helipad. His response was filled with warmth and familiarity, "Oh, that's quite far from the temple. Whenever I come here, I always opt for accommodation next to the sacred grounds." Despite being aware of his frequent visits, I couldn't resist asking, "Do you often come here?" He replied with a gentle nod and extended a heartfelt invitation to his own hotel for evening tea. He emphasized that I should come as a friend, leaving behind the role of a journalist confined to my own lodging. His simplicity and down-to-earth nature were so endearing that I momentarily forgot about the interview that initially brought us together.

As the evening cast its gentle glow, I made my way to Abhimanyu's hotel, conveniently nestled just beside the temple on the right side. Approaching the reception, I inquired about Mr. Abhimanyu, and the young attendant's face brightened with recognition. "Ah, Mr. Gaurav, he has been expecting you. His room number is

102," he informed me kindly. Dialing his room, the receptionist let Abhimanyu know of my arrival.

Stepping into his room, I was greeted with a warmth that instantly put me at ease. My eyes wandered and landed upon the captivating sight of several canvases scattered about. Notably, a canvas stood proudly on a stand in the balcony, capturing the essence of the temple. From this vantage point, the temple stood in all its glory, its majestic presence mere steps away from the hotel. The sight tugged at my heart, and a question brimmed within me.

Unable to contain my curiosity, I mustered the courage to inquire, "You mentioned that you visit Kedarnath often. As a painter, I assume you must have painted the Kedarnath temple before." His response held a sense of familiarity and devotion that left me awestruck. "Yes, every year I paint a rendition of the temple. This is my 20th painting of Kedarnath temple," he revealed.

I couldn't help but be taken aback. "For the past 20 years, you have been coming here?" I questioned, astonishment lacing my words. The magnitude of his commitment and dedication washed over me, leaving me in awe of his unwavering devotion.

As he replied, his voice carried a mixture of nostalgia and longing. "Well, actually it has been 23 years, but there were three years in between when I couldn't make it here." His eyes seemed to gaze into the past, reliving the memories. "In 2013, there was a devastating natural calamity that struck this place, and I couldn't come. And then, unfortunately, I was caught up with some assignments on two other occasions." His tone held a hint of disappointment.

A wave of emotions washed over me as I listened to his words. I could sense the deep regret he felt for those missed years. It was as if life had conspired against him, yet his determination remained unyielding. "But, you know," he continued, his voice tinged with a mix of gratitude and amazement, "despite the challenges, every year I try my best to come here." His unwavering devotion shone through his words.

In that moment, I couldn't help but admire his resilience. Here was a man who had faced obstacles and setbacks, yet his love for this place propelled him forward. The thought struck me: what a stroke of luck, or perhaps it was a testament to the grace of God, that our paths had crossed. This year also seemed to be difficult as I was in Chicago for the last month and just after the Delhi exhibition, I am going to Japan. I thought what a lucky man I am or is God's grace on me that I met him.

In that moment, I began to understand the depth of Abhimanyu's connection to Kedarnath. It wasn't just an annual pilgrimage; it was a sacred tradition woven into the very fabric of his being. The act of capturing the temple's essence on canvas year after year was a testament to his profound reverence for this divine space.

"I said, '23 years, that's a long time. You are a true Shiva devotee, I believe,'" I remarked, my voice filled with admiration. A smile tugged at the corners of

Abhimanyu's lips as he nodded in agreement. "Yes, of course, I am. But there is some other reason as well," he replied, his tone carrying a hint of mystery.

As I was about to inquire about the elusive reason, the sound of the room bell pierced the air. Abhimanyu, standing near the balcony, gestured for me to answer the door. It was the room service, delivering the tea he had ordered earlier. As we settled back into the conversation, the warmth of the tea cup in my hands creating a comforting ambiance, I couldn't contain my curiosity any longer. I wanted to delve deeper into his story, to understand him on a more personal level. So, I gently prodded, "You mentioned that there is some other reason for coming here."

Abhimanyu's reply caught me off guard, and a flush of embarrassment swept over me. "I wasn't telling you, my friend. I was merely mentioning it. I thought you had left the journalist at your hotel," he stated, his voice tinged with a mix of disappointment and trust. The realization hit me that I had unintentionally breached his trust. I quickly apologized, assuring him that I had no intention of conducting an interview.

In that moment, I wanted to make amends and regain his trust. I wanted him to understand that my intentions were pure, driven by genuine curiosity and a desire to connect. Sipping the tea, I mustered the sincerity in my voice as I explained, "I'm truly sorry. It was a random question, and I assure you, I am not here to exploit your story. I am here to listen, to understand, and to appreciate the depth of your connection with this place."

His eyes softened, and a flicker of understanding crossed his face. It was as if he could see the sincerity in my words. And in that exchange, a fragile bond of trust began to mend, reminding me of the importance of respecting boundaries and nurturing connections built on authenticity.

He laughed, a warm and genuine sound that eased the tension in the room. "Don't be embarrassed," he reassured me. "I was just joking. I understand that questioning people is your profession, and you must be quite used to it." His words carried a sense of lightheartedness, breaking the seriousness that had momentarily clouded our interaction.

Relieved by his understanding, I took a deep breath and shared a bit of my own story. "Honestly, this is my first project where I have to interview someone," I confessed. "My core area of work is advertising creatives. When I saw the advertisement for your exhibition, I was truly amazed by the creativity of the blurred half-finished portrait you used for the advertising campaign. It's brilliant." A genuine admiration shone through my words, reflecting the profound impact his art had on me.

From that moment, my admiration for you grew, and I became an ardent fan of your work. When I learned that someone from our office would be conducting an interview with you, I seized the opportunity. I pleaded with my boss, repeatedly requesting to be the one assigned to this task. After numerous appeals, he finally agreed, recognizing my genuine passion for your art and the opportunity for me to connect with you on a deeper level.

In that exchange, a shared enthusiasm and appreciation for art bridged the gap between us. I could see a glimmer of appreciation in Abhimanyu's eyes, a realization that our encounter was not just another interview, but a meeting of two individuals brought together by a shared love for creativity. It was a moment of connection, where the lines between interviewer and interviewee blurred, replaced by a mutual respect for each other's crafts.

Abhimanyu's brow furrowed, a mix of confusion and curiosity etched on his face. "Seriously, this is your first interview?" he questioned, his voice filled with disbelief. "And why would you want to interview me? You mentioned you've never done it before, right?"

I nodded, feeling a touch of nervousness. "Yes, it's true that I've never conducted an interview before, but I have assisted my colleagues a few times," I admitted, trying to ease his skepticism. The truth was, my experience was limited, but my determination to uncover the essence behind his artwork was unwavering.

I took a deep breath, mustering the courage to explain my intentions. "When I first saw the advertisement for your exhibition, I was immensely impressed by the theme. You see, this is my core field," I said, my voice filled with passion. "At first, I thought it was just a captivating design, but as I delved deeper into researching about you, I discovered that it is not just a design. It is your signature painting, a piece that you carry with you to every exhibition, and it's never up for sale."

Pausing for a moment, I met Abhimanyu's gaze. "What struck me the most," I continued, my voice tinged with emotion, "is that you have never used this painting as an advertising theme. So, naturally, a question arose in my mind: why now? That's the reason I wanted to conduct this interview, just to understand why now?"

A sense of vulnerability crept into my words as I confessed, "I know many people have asked you about the story behind this painting, and I'm sure there must be a story. I couldn't help but wonder if you had finally completed the painting and wanted to reveal it to the world, as it bears the caption 'Hope to complete it soon.'"

Regret washed over me as I realized my mistake. "I'm truly sorry," I apologized sincerely. "You specifically told me not to start the interview, and here I am, doing exactly that." I hoped my genuine remorse would convey my earnestness to respect his wishes and delve into the heart of the matter at hand.

He listened to me intently, his eyes filled with a calmness that seemed to hold the weight of years gone by. Sipping his tea, he savored the moment before turning his gaze towards the temple. A hint of nostalgia colored his voice as he began to share his thoughts.

"You know," he spoke softly, his words tinged with a mix of reflection and gratitude, "I believe that some things in life remain incomplete. That's why I come here every year, to visit Baba, because everything I have achieved today, this art, this fame, this wealth, it's all because of Lord Shiva." A profound sense of humility radiated from him as he acknowledged the divine role in his journey.

His gaze lingered on the temple, as if seeking solace and guidance. "But there is someone else who also played a part," he continued, his voice filled with a touch of mystery. "Every year, I express my gratitude to Lord Shiva here, and I come in the hope of meeting that other person, to personally thank them."

A wistful sigh escaped his lips as he spoke of his chosen artwork for the advertisement. "I don't even know why I chose that particular picture this time. Perhaps now, after all these years, my patience has found an answer," he confessed. "When I began creating that painting, I held the hope that I would complete it soon. But it has been 23 years since I started, and still, I haven't been able to complete it."

A heavy silence enveloped the room, the weight of Abhimanyu's unspoken emotions palpable in the air. I, too, remained quiet, realizing that I had touched upon a deeply personal and emotionally charged part of his life. The vulnerability etched across his face made me pause, allowing the moment to linger in the heaviness of unspoken words.

After what felt like an eternity, I mustered the courage to break the silence. "I'm sorry," I murmured, my voice filled with genuine remorse. "I seem to have delved into a sensitive topic." Abhimanyu shook his head gently, a mixture of sadness and understanding in his eyes. "It's not that I don't want to share or that no one knows about that picture," he replied softly. "I have a few friends who are aware, but I have made a promise to myself that when the painting is completed, I will present it to the person it belongs to. I will express my gratitude and let the whole world know that this person has been the driving force behind my artistic journey and everything I have become."

A sense of intrigue stirred within me as I listened to his words. There was an important person, someone who held great significance in his life. Gathering my courage, I ventured further. "If you don't mind," I began hesitantly, "may I ask a question ? “Abhimanyu chuckled, a touch of sarcasm in his voice, and replied, "Ah, let's continue with the interview, shall we?" The sarcastic laughter masked a deeper emotion, leaving me curious yet respectful of his boundaries.

What I admired most about Abhimanyu was his ability to infuse lightness into serious discussions. It was a quality that made him endearing. I couldn't help but comment, a chuckle escaping my lips, "Usually, when a relationship doesn't work out or a boyfriend gets dumped, they create such paintings." I said this in jest, hoping to bring a touch of humor to our conversation.

As the discussion continued, the sun gradually set, casting a dusky hue over the surroundings. Lost in our conversation, I hadn't realized how late it had become. It was then that Abhimanyu suggested we have dinner together. Delighted by the invitation, I eagerly agreed, realizing it was an opportunity to delve deeper into his life and learn more about him. We shared a meal, engaging in lively conversation that allowed me to gain further insights into his thoughts and experiences.

After dinner, we ventured out for a walk, immersing ourselves in the lively atmosphere. It became evident that Abhimanyu was well-known in this place. We encountered familiar faces everywhere we went — shopkeepers, restaurant owners, and acquaintances. It became clear that his regular visits to this place had formed lasting connections, turning strangers into friends.

As we strolled along, enjoying each other's company, Abhimanyu turned to me and asked, "When are you planning to go back?"

"I have seen Bholenath, I have met you, what else could I ask for?" I expressed, a mix of gratitude and contentment coloring my words. "So, I am considering heading back tomorrow. I had taken a few days off, but there is a mountain of pending work awaiting me. Moreover, I need to coordinate with your team as well."

Abhimanyu's smile illuminated his face as he responded, "Well, now I have something for you. Let's meet tomorrow at 4:30 in the morning." With those words, he turned and made his way into the hotel. I didn't question him further; instead, I headed back to my own hotel room.

Tossing and turning, sleep eluded me that night. My mind raced with thoughts of what to say, how to ask about his story, and how to unravel the mysteries behind his artwork. The weight of curiosity and the need for answers burdened my thoughts. However, the next day was fast approaching, and with an early morning wake-up call, I eventually succumbed to slumber.

2nd October

Morning arrived, accompanied by the piercing sound of the alarm clock. Groggily, I woke from my sleep, my mind still grappling with a mix of anticipation and uncertainty. Today held the promise of unraveling the enigma surrounding Abhimanyu's life, yet I couldn't help but feel a twinge of nervousness as I readied myself to meet him.

With a sense of purpose, I made my way to our designated meeting spot, my heart pounding with a mixture of excitement and trepidation. Little did I know that this early morning rendezvous would mark the beginning of a journey that would forever alter my perspective and leave an indelible imprint on my soul.

As I reached the temple, having taken a refreshing bath, I found Abhimanyu waiting for me in the tranquil courtyard. He suggested we first have darshan, seeking the divine blessings, before indulging in tea. We immersed ourselves in the morning aarti, the air filled with sacred chants and the aroma of incense. Afterward, Abhimanyu led me to the backside of the temple, a place that held a special significance to him.

As we ordered tea, he reached into his pocket, pulled out a piece of paper, and looked at me with a gentle smile. Carefully unfolding it, he placed it before me. It was a depiction of the Kedarnath temple, featuring two girls and a small child captured from the perspective of their backs. The sketch bore the markings of a beginner, exhibiting a rawness that contrasted with Abhimanyu's reputation as a brilliant artist.

I couldn't help but express my surprise, exclaiming, "This cannot be yours! You are such a talented artist." Doubt filled my voice, unable to reconcile the artwork before me with the masterpieces he had created.

With a humble smile, Abhimanyu responded, his words carrying wisdom and understanding, "Every professional was once a beginner, and so was I." His simple yet profound statement reminded me of the journey we all undertake to hone our skills and become who we are meant to be.

Without prompting, Abhimanyu offered to share a story, sensing the curiosity radiating from me. In that moment, the world around us seemed to fade away, leaving only his voice and the anticipation of the tale he was about to reveal. It was a moment brimming with emotion, as I leaned in, ready to listen with an open heart, eager to uncover the depths of his artistic journey.

Abhimanyu began speaking, his voice growing reflective as he shared a story from his past.

"This story goes back to 2001, when I had just graduated from school. I wanted to take a trip before starting college, and after hearing so much about Kedarnath, I decided to make that my destination. People often described it as a place of serenity and beauty, a place where, upon leaving, you felt as if you had been touched by something divine, as if you had momentarily stepped into heaven itself. I was excited, eager to see it with my own eyes." Abhimanyu's gaze turned distant as he continued, his mind clearly drifting back to that time. "I took a bus from Dehradun to Rishikesh, and then another to Kedarnath. The journey was long, but the closer I got, the more eager I became. And that's when I met Arun, a fellow traveler who was also on his way to Kedarnath. His village was just before the town, and his family lived and worked there during the six-month tourist season. He and I struck up a conversation during the long bus ride, and by the time we reached Kedarnath, we had become good friends." Abhimanyu smiled at the memory, a quiet fondness in his expression. "I had initially planned the trip with a friend, but at the last moment, my friend couldn't join. So, I ended up traveling alone. Arun and I shared stories during the journey, and when we arrived, he invited me to stay at his house in Kedarnath. At first, I hesitated—Kedarnath was a place I'd never been before, and staying with strangers felt uncertain. But Arun insisted, and after a little back and forth, I agreed." He paused, his fingers tracing the edge of the sketch as if recalling the small details that made the experience vivid. "When I think of it now, it feels like it was fate. The house where I stayed back then is now a government guest house, transformed after the 2013 disaster, but whenever I visit, I always try to stay in the same place. It brings back so many memories—memories of that first trip, the quiet stillness of the mountains, and the connection I had with the people there.

Abhimanyu's voice grew softer, his eyes distant as he leaned back, letting the memory carry him to a place where the past felt as vivid as the present.

"My first day in Kedarnath was nothing short of enchanting. The air was crisp, the scent of pine and earth mingled with the cool mountain breeze, and the majestic peaks that loomed above seemed to cradle the town in a protective embrace. Arun, being a local, made everything so much easier. The priests and temple staff knew him by name, and the warmth of their recognition allowed us to bypass the long lines of pilgrims. While others stood under the scorching sun, waiting their turn, we slipped through the back gate, entering the temple without a single glance at the crowded queue. We had darshan with an ease that felt almost sacred, as though the divine had opened its doors just for us."

A smile tugged at Abhimanyu's lips as he continued, the memory of those days in Kedarnath still fresh in his mind.

"I had spent four or five days there by then, and every day felt like a gift. Arun took me to places few visitors ever got to see, each one more breathtaking than the last. The crystal-clear streams that gurgled down the mountainside, the hidden shrines tucked away in forgotten corners of the valley, the eerie quiet of the mountains at dawn—everything was so perfect, so untouched. It was as if time had slowed down in Kedarnath, and the weight of the world had no place there."

“In the evenings, I would sit with the sages, their faces weathered by time and wisdom. They shared stories—tales of the temple’s creation, the miracles of Lord Shiva, the deep spiritual significance that reverberated through these mountains. I was entranced, hanging on every word. And as they spoke, I felt as though I were being woven into the fabric of the place itself. Each story added another layer to my understanding, each prayer and chant that filled the air seemed to seep into my soul, bringing a peace I had never known.”

He paused for a moment, his expression turning more introspective, and the room grew quieter as he relived the emotions of that time.

"I didn’t want to leave. I truly didn’t. Every corner of Kedarnath felt like it had cast its spell on me. The thought of leaving felt like being pulled away from something sacred, like being torn from heaven itself and cast back into the harshness of the world. It wasn’t just a place; it was a feeling—a divine embrace that I didn’t want to let go of. I found myself wishing that time could stop, that I could stay here forever, surrounded by the mountains and the peace that seemed to breathe through the very air."

“But, as with all things, time moved on. That evening, as I sat with Arun over dinner, I told him I was planning to leave the next day. He looked at me with surprise, his voice filled with concern. 'Why so soon?' he asked. 'Stay for a few more days.' I explained that my vacation was almost over, and I had to return to secure my college admission. But as fate would have it, sometimes the universe has a way of steering us in unexpected directions."

Abhimanyu's voice dropped to a thoughtful whisper as he shared the turning point.

"Arun told me that the next day, a major religious ceremony was taking place—something truly special, something I could never have imagined. He urged me to stay, to witness the ceremony, to be a part of something much greater than I could have anticipated. 'Just one more day,' he said. 'Don't miss it.'"

Abhimanyu let out a quiet laugh, as if recalling how small the decision seemed in the moment, but how significant it became.

"I thought about it, just for a second. One more day wouldn't hurt, I reasoned. And so, I decided to stay, knowing that sometimes, the most important moments in life happen when you least expect them.

The first time I saw her – 1st Encounter

Abhimanyu's voice softened as he continued, his expression shifting into something more personal, more intimate, as though he were reliving that very moment.

"The next day, I found myself sitting outside on the terrace, with a perfect view of the temple. Arun's house, nestled right next to the sacred site, allowed me to look out at the sea of devotees standing in long lines, all waiting for their turn to enter the temple. The sun was high in the sky, casting a warm golden hue over the scene. The air was filled with the soft murmur of prayers, the faint sound of bells from the temple, and the rustle of movement as people slowly made their way forward. It was a peaceful, ordinary morning, until my eyes locked onto her."

"There she was, amidst the crowd, standing out in a way that no one else did. I can't explain it exactly—there was something about the way she moved, the way the light seemed to catch her face—but in that instant, she felt like the most extraordinary thing in the world. She was incredibly beautiful. I couldn't take my eyes off her. She was just about to enter the temple, and I managed to catch only a fleeting glimpse of her face. But in that brief moment, something shifted inside me. It was like what people call 'love at first sight'—a feeling so sudden, so intense, it left me breathless."

He let out a small sigh, as if remembering the rush of emotions that had flooded over him.

"Without wasting a moment, I jumped to my feet and rushed downstairs, my heart pounding. I needed to see her again. My mind raced with thoughts of how I might meet her, maybe even speak to her. I had planned to enter the temple through the back gate, as I had done before, but just as I reached the bottom of the stairs, Arun's father stopped me. He reminded me about the special ceremony that was taking place that day, cautioning me not to wander off. His words delayed me for ten minutes, and in those ten minutes, the moment seemed to slip away, as if fate were teasing me."

Abhimanyu's hand gestured lightly, as if trying to grasp the fleeting feeling of that lost chance.

"Finally, after what seemed like an eternity, I made my way to the back gate. The guards, recognizing me from the past few days of visiting with Arun, let me through without hesitation. My heart raced as I entered the temple grounds, my eyes scanning the crowd for her. But she was nowhere to be found. She must have already finished her darshan and left, I thought, disappointment creeping in. I searched the area outside the temple, hoping for a glimpse of her, but the crowd had thinned, and she was nowhere to be seen."

"Frustrated, I gave up the search and spent the rest of the day attending the ceremony, but my thoughts were elsewhere. The event, as meaningful as it was, seemed distant and far less important now. All I could think of was her. That fleeting moment, that single glance, had captivated me in a way I couldn't shake."

He paused, a small smile playing at the corners of his lips as he recalled the next part of the story.

"In the evening, after the ceremony, Arun and I sat at a small tea shop near the house, sipping our tea and talking idly. And then, as if the universe had conspired to give me another chance, she appeared. It was her—the same girl from the morning! But this time, she was even more stunning up close. If she had been beautiful from a distance, now, in the soft evening light, she was nothing short of breathtaking."

"She had come with her younger brother, and they were buying some biscuits and snacks. I couldn't take my eyes off her. I watched as she carefully selected the items, her face radiant, her movements graceful. I even bought a chocolate for her brother, though I'm not sure she noticed. The whole time, I couldn't look away. Her face... it captivated me completely. I don't think I've ever been so mesmerized by someone's presence."

"After she gathered her things and left, I remained at the tea shop, but it felt as if my heart had gone with her. I stayed there, but she had already taken a part of me with her. And in that moment, I realized—she had become my everything in a way that words could never describe.

Abhimanyu's voice grew quiet as he continued, each word carrying the weight of a memory that had stayed with him for years.

"That night, her face stayed with me. It was as if it had imprinted itself on my mind. I couldn't stop thinking about her—about how beautiful she was, about what it would be like to talk to her. Would I see her again? If I did, what would I say? The thought of her consumed me, and no matter how hard I tried, sleep wouldn't come. My mind raced with questions and emotions, until, finally, exhaustion took over, and I drifted into a restless sleep."

He paused, letting the memory settle in, before continuing.

Day 2

"The next morning, Arun woke me up early. He told me, 'Brother, Dad is heading to the village. You can leave with him, and he'll help you catch a bus to Rishikesh.' But as he spoke, all I could think about was leaving. I didn't want to go, not yet. The thought of leaving without seeing her again was unbearable. So, I quickly came up with an excuse. 'Since Uncle is leaving, I think I'll stay here for a few more days,' I told him, trying to sound casual. But the truth was, it was her. I couldn't leave until I had one more chance to see her."

"After Arun's father left, I freshened up, though my mind was already on her. I went back to the terrace, hoping against hope that I'd catch another glimpse of her. And after some time, my heart leaped in my chest when I saw her again—standing in the darshan line, her younger brother by her side. Since Arun's house was right next to the temple, I had a clear view of the people waiting in line. She had been there for a while, patiently waiting her turn, when, almost as if on cue, her eyes met mine."

"I couldn't believe it. I had been watching her, and when she glanced at me again, I knew she had noticed. You know how it is—when you look at someone for long enough, they eventually catch you staring. And she did. She kept glancing back at me, and I could feel my heart racing. I don't know if she recognized me from the day before or if she was just curious, but there was something in her gaze. Something that made my chest tighten with hope."

He let out a breath, as if feeling the weight of that moment once more.

"Finally, her turn came, and she entered the temple. Without wasting a second, I rushed down, hoping to follow her. I made my way to the back gate, where the guards, once again, let me in without hesitation. The air seemed to hum with anticipation as I entered the temple, my eyes searching for her. And then I saw her—standing near the entrance, her presence like a magnet drawing me in. But it was what happened next that changed everything."

Abhimanyu's face softened, and a smile tugged at his lips as he recalled the moment that had stayed with him all these years.

"When she saw me—someone who had been sitting outside only moments before—something shifted. Her expression softened, and she smiled at me. It was the kind of smile that could melt the hardest of hearts. In that single moment, everything around me faded away. The people, the sounds—it all disappeared. It was just her, and that smile. That smile, that feeling, it's etched in my heart even after 23 years, as vivid as if it happened just yesterday."

"I'll never forget that smile. It felt like the world had paused for us, as if time itself had stopped to let that moment linger. It was the beginning of something I didn't yet understand, but it was a moment that would shape everything to come.

"After the darshan, she sat nearby, speaking with a sage. I found myself watching her from a distance, unable to gather the courage to approach. Normally, I wasn't the type to shy away from a conversation, but something about her made me nervous, almost paralyzed. I just didn't know what to say, or how to say it. Every time I thought about walking over to her, the words seemed to get lost in my mind. I was scared of making a fool of myself."

"She stayed there for a while, and I kept watching, unable to tear my eyes away. And then, she left. As she walked away, I couldn't help but follow her with my gaze. She glanced back a couple of times, and each time, I smiled, feeling a rush of happiness. It was a small, fleeting interaction, but it meant the world to me—at least she had noticed me. That tiny acknowledgment made my heart flutter in a way I couldn't explain."

Abhimanyu exhaled slowly, as if recalling the tension of the afternoon.

"Later that afternoon, Arun and I were standing behind the temple, just enjoying the weather. The morning had been rainy, but now the sun had come out, bathing the mountains in golden light. Arun had brought some books, and we were both soaking in the warmth, taking a moment to relax. But then, out of the corner of my eye, I saw her again. She had come and sat down some distance away, with a young local girl beside her."

He smiled at the memory, a quiet amusement in his tone.

"That whole afternoon felt like something out of a dream. We kept stealing glances at each other, eyes meeting for just a moment before quickly darting away, neither of us making a move to speak. There was an unspoken connection between us, an invisible thread pulling us together, but neither of us knew how to reach across it. It was as if we were both waiting for the other to take the first step, but neither of us had the courage."

Abhimanyu chuckled softly to himself, shaking his head as he recalled his next impulsive decision.

"I don't know what came over me, but all of a sudden, I grabbed a notebook from Arun's bag and started sketching something. Arun raised an eyebrow and asked, 'What are you doing?' I didn't want to admit the truth, so I just said, 'Nothing, just sketching the mountains.' But deep down, I knew. I wasn't drawing the mountains. I was trying to impress her. I'd never really drawn before, but in that moment, I felt this overwhelming urge to capture something on paper. And so, with every glance at her, I tried to sketch her presence, her face, though I could never truly capture the beauty of it. It wasn't the mountains I was drawing—it was her, in my own way."

"I don't know if she ever saw me drawing, but every time I looked up, I'd catch her gaze again. We shared those quiet moments, those stolen glances, and somehow, it felt like enough. For the first time, I wasn't worried about what to say—I was just trying to savor the moment, to hold on to the feeling of being close to her, even if it was only through a simple sketch.

"Page after page went to waste—I couldn't get it right. No matter how hard I tried, the lines seemed to blur, and the image wouldn't form. I could feel her watching me from afar, and I couldn't shake the feeling that she had noticed my futile attempts. I saw her smile, and I knew—she probably understood exactly what I was up to. The realization made me feel both exposed and vulnerable, but I couldn't stop.

A little while later, she stood up, and my heart skipped a beat. She started walking toward us, and suddenly, I felt an overwhelming wave of nervousness and embarrassment. It was as though the ground beneath me had disappeared, and I couldn't even bring myself to look at her. My gaze stayed fixed on the notebook, my fingers trembling slightly as I tried to focus.

With my head still down, I whispered to Arun, almost too afraid to speak. 'Is she coming this way?'

He glanced up and nodded. 'Yes.'

'Is she looking at us?' I asked, unable to keep the panic from creeping into my voice.

'Yes,' Arun replied, his voice calm but knowing.

That only made me more anxious. My mind raced—what if she said something? What would I say? The questions swirled in my head, each one more suffocating than the last. I could feel my palms growing clammy.

Moments later, she was standing right in front of us, the younger girl still by her side. My heart was thumping in my chest, and I could hardly breathe. She turned to the younger girl and spoke, her voice clear and calm.

'A person should keep trying—only then can they succeed. And if the effort is made with God's blessing, it's bound to succeed.' Her words were simple, yet somehow, they felt profound, like they were meant for me. I felt a deep, almost spiritual shift within me, as if the universe was aligning in that very moment.

She smiled, and then, as quickly as she had come, she turned and walked away. I was left speechless, my heart racing, my mind a whirl of emotions. Her words lingered in the air, and I couldn't shake the feeling that they had been meant for me. I wanted to call out, but the moment was already slipping away, and I was left standing there, breathless.

Arun had been watching all of this unfold, and though I hadn't said much, he seemed to understand. He looked at me knowingly and said, 'She didn't directly talk to you, but her words were definitely meant for you.' I nodded. It felt like the truth, a truth I couldn't quite explain, but felt deep in my bones.

That was the first day I tried to sketch the temple. I spent hours on it, trying to capture the essence of the place—the majesty, the stillness—but nothing seemed to turn out right. I couldn't stop thinking about her, about her words. They had planted a seed of hope in me, and I couldn't let go of that feeling.

As the evening drew near, we went back to the house. Later, we sat at the tea stall below, sipping our tea in silence. The warm, rich aroma of it filled the air, but my mind was elsewhere. For some reason, I had this strange gut feeling that she would come there again. I don't know how or why, but I couldn't shake it.

And just as I had hoped, she did.

She came again, this time with the same girl as before, and they bought some chips. Arun nudged me, urging me to speak to her, but every time I saw her, I froze. It wasn't fear exactly—it was more like being completely mesmerized. My mind raced with words, but they got caught in my throat. I couldn't gather the courage to speak to her. It felt like my world had narrowed down to that one moment, that one feeling of being completely spellbound.

As she was about to leave, the sky darkened, and a light drizzle began to fall. The gentle patter of raindrops, mixed with the faint sound of the wind, created a peaceful atmosphere. Around the same time, a group of traveling musicians arrived, carrying their instruments. They set up near the tea stall, and soon, the sweet melodies of a flute and harmonium filled the air. The setting was something straight out of a dream—the twilight glowing softly in the background, a thin veil of snow surrounding the place, the light drizzle falling like mist over the world, and the steam rising from the clay cups of tea. In the center, a small fire flickered, casting a warm glow. Through the dancing flames, her face shone like it was touched by some ethereal light. It felt surreal, almost cinematic, as if I was living inside a movie scene.

I didn't know what to do, so I hatched a plan. Since I couldn't bring myself to speak to her, I decided to communicate through songs. I turned to the musicians and, gathering all the courage I could, requested them to play 'Ek Ajnabee Haseena Se Yun Mulakat Ho Gayi.' As the first notes of the song floated through the air, I saw her glance at me. And in that fleeting moment, she immediately looked down, blushing. I knew then—she understood. She knew exactly what I was trying to convey.

When the song ended, I didn't hesitate. I quickly requested another song: 'Khwaab Ho Tum Ya Koi Haqeeqat.' The musicians didn't know the song well, so I began to sing it myself, my voice trembling with emotion. The moment I started, they joined in, adding their melody to mine. I could feel her gaze on me the entire time, the weight of it sending chills down my spine. When the song came to an end, I was already thinking of what song to ask for next, but before I could decide, she spoke.

'Can you sing this song, please?' she asked—not me directly, but the musicians.

The song she requested was 'Jaane Kaise Kab Aur Kahan Ikraar Ho Gaya.' As the first notes played, our eyes met, and time seemed to slow down. The world around us faded away—the drizzle, the musicians, the flickering fire—it was just the two of us, locked in that one moment. It was exactly like the kind of moment you see in the movies—intense, magical, and unforgettable.

In that moment, I felt something shift inside me, something deeper than just admiration. It was as if we had both silently acknowledged that something was unfolding between us, something inexplicable and beautiful, and it was all wrapped up in the music, the rain, and the stillness of the evening.

Abhimanyu's voice softened, as if he were still caught in the haze of that moment, reliving it with vivid clarity.

"As the final note of the song lingered in the air, the rain seemed to stop, as though the heavens had aligned with the stillness that surrounded us. The girl with her spoke up, breaking the spell. 'Didi, let's go now. It's getting late, and it might rain again.' She glanced at me briefly, her gaze lingering for a fraction of a second—almost as if she was waiting for some signal from me, as if asking whether she should stay or leave.

Before I could even gather my thoughts to respond, Arun's loud voice cut through the moment. 'Tomorrow at 11 a.m., we're heading to Bhairav Nath for darshan, and then to the top of the mountain for skiing. It's an amazing place, don't forget—sharp at 11!'

He repeated the time twice, his voice deliberate, and at first, I didn't understand why. I was still caught up in the moment, my heart beating too loudly to focus on anything else. But as she left with the younger girl, Arun leaned in and said, 'Bro, you're never going to talk to her on your own, are you?'

I sighed, my voice barely above a whisper. 'It's not that—I'm just trying to figure out if she's interested in talking to me or not.'

Arun's eyes gleamed with a knowing look. 'That's why I made sure she overheard our plan,' he said. 'If she's even a little interested, she'll show up tomorrow. And if she does, you better talk to her then. That other girl with her will definitely bring her along if she's interested.'

I couldn't help but smile at Arun's cleverness. It was his way of giving me a nudge, creating another chance, a new opportunity I might not have had otherwise. His confidence made me feel hopeful, as though fate itself had given me one last chance to make something happen.

I thanked Arun, feeling the weight of everything I had just experienced. We headed back to the house, and the evening passed in a blur of routine—dinner was cooked, we ate in silence, and yet my mind was trapped on one singular thought: Would she come tomorrow? If she did, what would I say? And if she didn't... well, then I would lose this fragile hope I had been holding on to all day.

Arun kept reassuring me, his voice steady and confident. 'Bro, I've seen her looking at you too. I'm telling you, she'll come.'

I wasn't so sure, but his words gave me something to hold on to, a glimmer of possibility. Maybe he was just trying to boost my confidence, or maybe he had seen something I hadn't.

As the night wore on, I found myself caught between the exhaustion of the day's adventures and the whirlwind of thoughts racing in my mind. Eventually, the fatigue won, and I drifted off to sleep, the hope of tomorrow still pulsing in my chest, a soft promise of what could be."

Abhimanyu paused for a moment, the weight of his words lingering in the air. His gaze seemed far away as if the memory had taken him back to that night, when hope and uncertainty mingled together under the cool, mountain sky.

Day 3

The next morning, I woke up early, completed my darshan at the temple, and returned to the rooftop. My eyes scanned the courtyard, searching for her among the devotees. Time felt like it was crawling as I waited, but she didn't come. A strange heaviness settled in my chest. She had been there every morning for the past two days—what could have kept her away today?

I kept glancing toward the temple, hoping to catch a glimpse of her, but the courtyard remained unchanged. As the minutes ticked by, an uneasy restlessness grew within me. My mind raced with questions. Had she already left Kedarnath? Or was something wrong?

"Bro, it's already 10:30!" Arun's voice broke through my thoughts. I turned to see him standing at the door. "We need to leave soon if we want to reach Bhairavnath by 11!"

I glanced at my watch and realized I'd lost track of time. I had been sitting there for hours, waiting, with no sign of her. Doubts filled my mind—would she come? Or was this it?

I quickly shook off my thoughts and got ready to leave. Arun and I started our walk to the Bhairavnath Temple, the sound of our footsteps crunching softly in the snow-covered path. The air was sharp and cold, but the breathtaking scenery distracted me momentarily. Towering peaks loomed in the distance, their snowcaps glowing in the morning light.

We reached the temple just in time, offered our prayers to Bhairav Baba, and then began climbing further up the mountain. With every step, the world seemed to grow quieter. The trail, though not very long, felt like a bridge to another world—a pristine, untouched expanse of white, where even the air seemed purer.

The view at the top was nothing short of magical. Snow stretched out endlessly in every direction, glimmering under the sunlight. The mountains stood tall and majestic, their silent beauty humbling yet awe-inspiring. I paused for a moment, taking in the serenity of it all, but my thoughts kept drifting back to her.

Had she stayed behind in the village? Or maybe she had left Kedarnath altogether? My chest tightened at the thought, and I found myself scanning the snowy trail below, hoping for some miracle.

I checked the time—it was 11:10. The silence of the place, broken only by the occasional rustling of leaves or the distant calls of birds, seemed to amplify my anticipation. But there was no sign of her. My heart grew heavier with each passing moment. What if she wasn't coming? What if I had misread the signs, and she wasn't interested at all?

11:10 turned into 11:30, and then 12:00. Each tick of the clock felt like another nail in the coffin of my hope. The pristine beauty of the snowy landscape that had mesmerized me earlier now seemed dull, overcast by disappointment.

Suddenly, the weather began to change. Dark clouds rolled in, and a cold gust of wind swept through, carrying the scent of impending rain. Within minutes, the heavens opened, unleashing a sudden downpour. There was no proper shelter around, so Arun and I huddled under the sparse cover of a rocky overhang and a tree. The rain was relentless, soaking through the branches above us.

The storm continued for nearly half an hour, drenching everything in sight. I looked out at the rain-drenched path, my heart sinking further. "In this weather, there's no chance she'll come," I muttered to myself.

Disheartened, I turned to Arun and said, "The rain has eased up. We should probably head back now."

Arun shrugged, clearly disappointed too, but just as we stepped out from under the tree, the rain began to lighten. A faint shaft of sunlight broke through the clouds, scattering golden light across the glistening snow. And then, as if summoned by that very light, she appeared.

She was with the same local girl as before, walking up the trail toward us. My breath caught at the sight of her. The light drizzle had left her hair damp, and droplets sparkled on her face like tiny jewels. The soft sunlight seemed to embrace her, making her look ethereal—like a vision out of a dream. Even today, I vividly remember that moment, and I still feel that all the waiting, the longing, was worth it.

As soon as her eyes met mine, she smiled and said to the girl beside her, "Sorry, if it hadn't rained, I would've arrived earlier." Though she was addressing her friend, I knew those words were meant for me. I smiled back, my heart racing.

She walked a little further and sat down on a smooth rock, visibly tired from the climb. She had brought a thermos of tea, likely because her friend had warned her about the lack of shops up here. The local girl turned to us and asked, "Would you like some tea?" Arun immediately accepted, and before I could even respond, she handed us two cups.

I held the warm cup in my hands, grateful for the tea but even more for the opportunity to be near her. My eyes kept drifting toward her, and I caught her stealing glances at me too. The connection was unspoken, yet palpable.

For a while, we simply sipped our tea in silence. My heart urged me to say something, anything, but the words wouldn't come. I've never thought of myself as shy, but in that moment, I was utterly tongue-tied. Every time I thought of starting a conversation, my mind blanked out.

Just as I finished my tea and resolved to at least thank her, a group of 15–20 people arrived. They were mostly older men and women, uncles and aunts, talking loudly and bustling around the small clearing. The moment was shattered. If I'd been nervous about talking to her before, the crowd made it feel downright impossible.

The group settled briefly, chatting and laughing, but soon the weather began to change again. The clouds darkened ominously, and the wind picked up, colder this time. Everyone agreed it was best to start heading back before the storm worsened. Reluctantly, I joined the descent, stealing glances at her whenever I could.

She walked with her friend a few steps ahead of me, occasionally turning back to look at me. Though we didn't exchange a single word after that brief smile, the way she looked at me felt like a conversation in itself.

Even as the path wound back down the mountain and the group dispersed, I found myself walking in silence, replaying every moment of the day in my mind.

As we were leaving, the girl with her spoke something to Arun in the local language. Curious, I watched as Arun turned to me with a grin. "She has a message for you," he said.

"A message?" I asked, my heart instantly racing.

"She said to meet her behind the temple at 5 pm," Arun replied, his tone teasing.

I froze for a moment, replaying those words in my head. This was it—the sign I had been waiting for, the confirmation that she wanted to talk to me as much as I wanted to talk to her. There was no longer any doubt.

We returned home, but my thoughts remained at the temple, already imagining what the meeting might be like. The climb had left me exhausted, and my eyelids were heavy, but I was too restless to sleep. What if I dozed off and missed her? What if she came and left, thinking I hadn't cared enough to show up?

I forced myself to stay awake, pacing around the room and rehearsing in my mind. How would I start the conversation? Should I compliment her first? Should I ask her name? I realized, with some embarrassment, that I didn't even know her name yet.

By 4 pm, I couldn't sit still anymore. I started getting ready, taking extra care with my appearance. Every second felt like an eternity, but by 4:30, I was already heading toward the temple. I wanted to be there early—not just to ensure I didn't miss her but also to calm my nerves before she arrived.

I still remember the words I practiced over and over in my head. I would tell her, "I have never seen anyone more beautiful than you," and then I'd ask for her name. I repeated the line so many times that it felt like second nature by the time I reached the temple.

The minutes ticked by slowly as I waited, my heart beating faster with each passing moment. Exactly at 5 pm, I saw her. She was walking toward me, and my heart began to race uncontrollably. This was the moment I had been anticipating all day.

I started walking toward her, trying to summon every ounce of courage I had. But just as I got a little closer, she subtly signaled with her hand for me to stop and stay quiet. Confused, I froze, and then she motioned for me to look behind her.

When I turned my gaze, I saw them—an older man and woman, accompanied by a young boy. My heart sank as the realization hit me. These were her parents, and the boy was her younger brother, the same one I had bought chocolate for the other day.

I had been so focused on her that I hadn't even noticed the others walking with her. Her timely gesture saved me from a potential disaster—I couldn't imagine what might have happened if I had approached her in front of her family.

We passed each other in silence, as if we were strangers. But in that fleeting moment, as our eyes met, an unspoken understanding passed between us. It wasn't the meeting I had imagined, yet I felt a strange sense of connection, as though this silent exchange had said more than words ever could.

As I walked away, my mind was racing again, but this time it wasn't with disappointment. It was with hope.

Abhimanyu paused, his gaze fixed on something distant, as though the memories he was recounting had taken him back in time. The silence between us was heavy, yet brimming with unspoken emotions.

I didn't know how to respond, but I knew I had to say something. Breaking the silence, I asked, "Then what happened next?"

Abhimanyu looked at me, his expression a mix of nostalgia and pain. "The next day, I waited again for her," he said softly. "First at the temple in the morning, and later at the tea shop, hoping she'd come. But she didn't. By evening, I couldn't contain my restlessness anymore and decided to ask the girl who was always with her." He paused, his voice faltering slightly.

"What did she say?" I asked, leaning forward instinctively.

"She told me that... she had left," Abhimanyu replied, his voice barely above a whisper. "She had to return home and wouldn't be coming back. That girl also mentioned that she had written her phone number down to pass it on to me, but the paper somehow got lost. Just like that, she slipped out of my life as suddenly as she had entered it."

He smiled faintly, but it was a smile tinged with sadness. "And that, Gaurav, is the story behind the unfinished portrait."

For a moment, I couldn't find my voice. The weight of his words and the simplicity of his confession left me stunned. It was difficult to comprehend how someone could be so profoundly affected by such fleeting encounters. After a pause, I hesitantly asked, "You remember every moment, every glance, every detail of those three days. Yet, why couldn't you complete that portrait? Why leave it unfinished?"

Abhimanyu turned to me, his eyes reflecting a mixture of longing and conviction. "I could have completed it anytime," he said. "It wasn't necessary for her to be present. Her face is etched in my mind as vividly as it was that first day. But my wish has always been that whenever I meet her again—if fate allows—I'll finish it then.

"Now, after so many years, she must be someone's wife, living her own life, perhaps with a family of her own. If I were to complete the portrait now, it could cast a shadow on her reputation. That's something I could never allow. Maybe... maybe the destiny of that portrait was always to remain incomplete."

His words left me speechless. The depth of his feelings, his unwavering respect for her, and his selflessness were unlike anything I had ever encountered.

The next day, as we bid farewell, I felt a strange sense of reverence for Abhimanyu. We promised to meet again at the exhibition before parting ways.

On the journey back to Delhi, my thoughts were consumed by the story he had shared. It amazed me how just three days—filled with little more than glances and unspoken words—had left such an indelible mark on Abhimanyu's heart. And even more remarkable was his decision to leave the portrait incomplete, not because he lacked the skill or inspiration, but because he valued her dignity above his own artistic fulfillment.

As I replayed his story in my mind, I couldn't help but think that Abhimanyu wasn't just a great artist; he was also a man of extraordinary character.

When I returned home, the first thing I did was share the news with Neha. "You won't believe it," I said, my voice brimming with excitement. "I met Abhimanyu in Kedarnath."

At first, Neha raised an eyebrow and gave me one of those skeptical smiles. "You're joking, right?" she said, shaking her head slightly.

"No, I'm serious," I insisted, recounting every detail of how our paths had crossed, how we had gradually become friends, and how Abhimanyu had shared the poignant story behind his unfinished portrait. As I spoke, her expression changed from disbelief to intrigue.

To solidify my claim, I pulled out the paper Abhimanyu had given me—the rough sketch of the Kedarnath temple that he had drawn during one of our conversations. I handed it to her carefully, almost reverently.

Neha took the paper, examining the sketch with curiosity. "This is... beautiful," she murmured, tracing the delicate lines with her fingers. "So, you're not kidding. You really met him."

Her tone had shifted, and I could tell she was beginning to understand the significance of the encounter.

"Exactly," I said, encouraged by her response. "It was an incredible experience. He told me about this one girl he met years ago, who inspired his work, and how that inspiration has stayed with him all this time. You know, he's still waiting to finish the portrait because of her. Can you imagine?"

Neha's demeanor grew more serious. She placed the sketch carefully on the table, then leaned back in her chair, her brow furrowed in thought. "Three days?" she asked, her voice laced with disbelief. "He only saw her for three days, and that became his lifelong inspiration?"

I nodded, understanding her disbelief. "I had the same reaction when he told me. It's hard to grasp how such brief encounters can have such a lasting impact. But when you hear him speak about it... it feels real, Neha. It's like those moments with her were etched into his soul."

Neha didn't respond right away. She seemed lost in thought, her gaze fixed on the sketch as though it held answers to unspoken questions. I knew she wasn't particularly interested in art or cultural events, but something about Abhimanyu's story seemed to resonate with her.

Breaking the silence, I said, "You know, he personally invited us to his exhibition. He asked me to come with the whole family." I hesitated for a moment before adding, "Would you like to join me?"

Neha looked up, a faint smile playing on her lips. "After hearing this story, how could I not? I'd love to meet someone like him."

Her answer filled me with a sense of fulfillment. I couldn't wait for the day of the exhibition—not just to see Abhimanyu again but to witness the world he had created through his art, inspired by a story that now felt as much a part of my life as his.

The Big Day

A few days later, we attended Abhimanyu's much-anticipated exhibition. It was a grand affair, buzzing with the hum of intellectual conversations and the soft strains of classical music. The gallery, with its soft, warm lighting, felt almost like a temple itself—each painting an offering of Abhimanyu's soul.

As soon as Abhimanyu saw me, he broke into a smile and walked over swiftly. He hugged me with genuine warmth. "Gaurav!" he said, his voice resonating with affection.

"This is Neha, my wife," I introduced her. "She's been eager to meet the man behind the portrait."

Abhimanyu turned to Neha. For the briefest moment, his calm demeanor faltered, his eyes reflecting a flash of something—recognition, maybe? Neha greeted him politely, but there was something in her voice, a faint tremor that only I caught.

After a few pleasantries, Abhimanyu excused himself to tend to the other guests. Neha turned to me, her curiosity unmistakable. "Where is it?" she asked, her voice low but insistent.

I knew what she meant. Without a word, I led her through the sea of onlookers and admirers to the secluded corner of the gallery. There it was—the unfinished masterpiece, standing apart from the others like an unresolved melody.

Even incomplete, the portrait had a magnetism that was hard to explain. The woman in the painting seemed to possess a timeless beauty, her half-drawn features speaking of a story untold. The strokes of Abhimanyu's brush captured not just her likeness but the very essence of her being—a spirit frozen in a moment of fleeting eternity.

As we stood before the painting, my phone buzzed, breaking the spell. It was a work call—urgent enough that I had to step outside to take it. I left Neha there, promising to return quickly.

When I came back, what I saw stopped me in my tracks. Neha stood motionless, her eyes locked onto the painting, her expression unreadable yet deeply intense. Abhimanyu stood a short distance away, watching her, his face calm but his eyes betraying a storm of emotions.

I approached cautiously, feeling like I was intruding on something far greater than myself. As I drew closer, Neha spoke, her voice barely above a whisper yet filled with meaning:

"What someone has truly said… if you try with the blessings of God, it will definitely be successful."

Her words sent a chill down my spine. They were the exact words—the same ones Abhimanyu had told me the girl had spoken to him that day in Kedarnath, when he had been sketching behind the temple.

Abhimanyu's lips curved into a faint, knowing smile. He turned to me, his gaze steady but gentle, and said, "Thank you, Gaurav," before walking away, leaving me standing there with Neha.

The weight of realization crashed over me like a wave, leaving me breathless. Those words, that look in Abhimanyu's eyes, and the way Neha gazed at the portrait—it all came together like pieces of a puzzle I hadn't even known I was solving.

I looked at Neha, my heart pounding. She said nothing more, but her face—calm, serene, and yet distant—revealed everything and nothing at the same time. She lingered in front of the portrait for a moment longer, then turned to me with a soft smile that carried the weight of unspoken truths.

Abhimanyu never displayed that portrait again. After the exhibition, it disappeared, as if it had retreated into the shadows of its own story. I never asked why, and neither did Neha. The questions I wanted to ask burned in my chest, but the answers felt too sacred, too fragile, to be voiced.

Perhaps the three of us knew the truth, but we chose to keep it locked away—a secret shared silently, bound by respect and an unexplainable understanding.

That portrait—unfinished yet eternal—became a metaphor for everything unsaid. Perhaps it was never meant to be completed, its beauty lying in its imperfection, in the echoes of a love that never fully blossomed. Or perhaps, in a way beyond comprehension, it was complete—a testament to a fleeting connection that transcended time, place, and even words.

Maybe the greatest masterpieces are the ones left unfinished.

Maybe...

Disclaimer

This is a work of fiction, created solely for the purpose of entertainment. Any names, characters, businesses, or locations mentioned within this story are entirely fictional. Any resemblance to actual persons, living or dead, or real events is purely coincidental.

The author intends no harm or offense through the content of this book. It is purely a product of imagination, meant to entertain and evoke emotions, without any intention of reflecting upon or portraying real-life individuals or occurrences.

The story, its characters, and all associated elements are a creation of the author's artistic expression, and any resemblance to real-life entities is not intentional.

Enjoy the journey, and thank you for reading.

Sneak Peek: Abhishek Bhatt's Next Book (Coming Soon)

What happens when two souls, destined to meet, are brought together by fate but separated by life's cruel twists?

Set against the vibrant backdrop of college life, "Abhishek's next book" captures the innocence, passion, and raw intensity of first love. It's a story of two individuals who, despite their differences, find an unexplainable connection in each other. As they navigate the highs of young love and the heartbreak of missed chances, they come to realize that destiny has its own plans.

This isn't just a love story—it's a tale of unforgettable regrets, bittersweet memories, and the paths we take when life demands us to choose. The characters grapple with the unpredictability of fate, the ache of unfulfilled dreams, and the question that haunts us all: What if?

In a world where not every love story ends with 'happily ever after,' this book explores the beauty of incomplete relationships, where the pain and lessons shape who we become.

With its raw emotions and deeply relatable moments, "Abhishek's next book" will make you laugh, cry, and reflect on the choices that define us. It's a journey of self-discovery, heartbreak, and hope—a story that lingers long after the last page is turned.

Prepare to be swept away by a tale where love, life, and destiny collide. Coming Soon!

For the Readers
Discussion Questions

The painter waited 20 years to complete a portrait of someone he met only for three days. What does this reveal about the nature of love, memory, and obsession? Can love be selfless, or does it sometimes border on idealization?

The "unfinished portrait" plays a central role in the story. What do you think it symbolizes beyond the painter's longing? Could it represent something larger, like unfulfilled potential or lost opportunities?

If you were in the painter's shoes, would you have waited so long to reconnect with someone? Or would you have chosen to move on? Why or why not?

The story beautifully highlights the power of fleeting moments. Can you recall a moment or a person in your life who left an indelible mark, even if they were only present for a short time?

Not every story has a perfect ending. Do you believe some relationships or experiences are meant to remain "unfinished"? Why or why not?

Insights from the Author

This story is more than just a tale about art, love, and longing—it's an exploration of time, memory, and the emotional truths that shape our lives. Through the painter's journey, I wanted to capture the complexity of human experience:

Time and Memory: How certain memories stay with us, refusing to fade, even as time passes.

Love and Longing: The way love can both uplift and torment us, and how longing can fuel both creation and destruction.

Closure vs. Continuity: Not every story in life gets wrapped up neatly with a conclusion. Some of the most powerful stories are the ones that remain open-ended.

I hope that you, as the reader, were able to feel the depth of these themes and reflect on how they resonate with your own life.

A Note for You

Dear Reader,

Thank you for choosing to spend your time with this story. The Unfinished Portrait is more than just a tale of love and longing—it's an exploration of the human experience. Through the painter's journey, I wanted to capture the emotions we all face at some point: the ache of unfulfilled dreams, the hope of a second chance, and the beauty in the moments we hold onto, even when they're fleeting.

This story is deeply personal to me, and I hope it touched your heart in the same way it touched mine while writing it. I believe that every reader will find a part of themselves within these pages. Perhaps you've had your own "unfinished portrait" in life—someone or something that left an indelible mark on your heart.

I would love to hear your reflections and interpretations of this story. What moments stood out to you? What did the "unfinished portrait" mean to you? And most importantly, what emotions did it evoke?

You can connect with me on social media to share your thoughts or simply drop me a message—I cherish every interaction with my readers. If this book inspired you, I encourage you to share it with others, as stories are meant to be passed on, to spark conversations, and to leave an impact.

Lastly, as you close this book, I hope it stays with you for a while, like a lingering melody that refuses to fade. And I hope it reminds you that, sometimes, it's the incomplete, unfinished moments in life that shape us the most.

With gratitude and warmth,

Abhishek Bhatt